... For more than a ~~~~ she had been on the ~~~~ point of some sort, a ~~~~ would recognize as such; surely it would come with the beginning of high school. Four years —only four more precious years—then what? College, that was what.

Nobody knew yet but Enie herself, her mind was made up; somehow or other she would manage to acquire enough education for a teacher's certificate. Nothing could hold her in Tired Creek then, nothing.

"I'm going to hit that big new highway and go," she muttered, tingling as she sent her broom in vigorous strokes across the porch. "I'm going up north and see snow, I'm going to see the ocean—and a mountain, a real mountain, so high you can look down into clouds from the top of it...."

Critics' Corner:

"A tremendously moving story of a young girl growing up in a poor Alabama farming community during the depression years. Every member of Enie's family is characterized with sharp clarity...."
—Bulletin of the Center for Children's Books

"...seldom does a book for older girls offer such perfect portrayal of characters and such perfect feeling for time and place. A story like this doesn't come along very often, but it stays for a long, long while."
—**Library Journal
(most highly recommended)

" 'It's a funny thing,' one young reader of Mildred Lee's *The Rock and the Willow* said, 'but Enie reminds me of Anne Frank.' In this perceptive comment lies the key to the extraordinary quality of this novel. It deals with difficult and somber facts, but its pages are so lit up with joy that the reader is moved rather than depressed.... Enie sees early all the facts of life, and her acceptance of them is part of her growing up. Her alert and creative mind is a bright spot on a dark landscape, but it is never sentimentalized.... In the end the most difficult thing that she has to accept is the incomprehensible fact that it is through trouble and suffering that good comes to her...."
—The New York Times

Other Recommendations: A.L.A. Booklist; Horn Book; H. W. Wilson Junior High School Catalog; Child Study Association of America Children's Book Award, 1963.

About the Author:

MILDRED LEE was born in Blockton, Alabama. She has three children and lives with her husband and daughter in St. Petersburg, Florida. Miss Lee says she has loved to read since childhood. She also enjoys "good" talk, singing, and exploring. About her writing, she says, "I get my characters from real people, of course, but never in their entirety. A bit here and there, from this person—maybe even a forgotten one about whom something may float up from the mists of subconscious—or from a member of my family. Anywhere and everywhere, but most of all out of my own head."

THE
ROCK

YP
Lee

Lee, Mildred

The rock and the willow

YP

LEE, MILDRED

The Rock and the Willow

THE ROCK AND THE WILLOW

Lothrop, Lee & Shepard edition published 1963

Archway Paperback edition published August, 1973

3rd printing....................November, 1973

Published by
POCKET BOOKS, a division of Simon & Schuster, Inc.,
630 Fifth Avenue, New York, N.Y.

Archway Paperback editions are distributed in the U.S.
by Simon & Schuster, Inc., 630 Fifth Avenue, New
York, N.Y. 10020, and in Canada by Simon & Schuster
of Canada, Ltd., Richmond Hill, Ontario, Canada.

L

Standard Book Number: 671-29502-0.
Library of Congress Catalog Card Number: 63-19689.

Printed in the U.S.A.

To Barbara, Bob and Janie

THE
ROCK
AND THE
WILLOW

1

THE RAIN started sometime in the night. Enie woke to hear its patter on the new tin roof Papa and the boys had put on two weeks ago. As he laid his tools away Papa had predicted darkly that likely there'd be a drought now to ruin his crops if he ever got the ground broken to put them in. He said the new roof was bad luck, but Mamma's jawing him about it all winter was enough to drive a man to anything.

Enie tried to shove Leeroy's moist little body to one side, but it was a dead weight in sleep and did not budge. She gave up and crawled closer to the edge of the mattress, settling herself as comfortably as she could. The room was warmer than when she had gone to bed and she gave the quilt a sleepy kick. In the same moment she knew what there was about this rain that was special. It was spring.

You could hear it in the rain and the erratic wind, and feel it in the new warmth of the room.

A gust of wind dashed the rain against the window and Leeroy cried out from a troubling dream. Enie touched him and he quieted. A shutter banged, the rain settled to a steady rattle on the tin roof, Enie's eyelids grew heavy and gritty. When she opened them, the sun was streaming in at the window and Leeroy was wandering about the room, muttering to himself. He stopped and stood still by the window, the sun struck gold across his body. His shoulder blades stood up like wings, his dark hair grew in tufts about his big ears and in a point down his thin neck.

Enie watched him wriggle into his patched overalls. She was about to roll over and sample the brief luxury of a whole bed when the wall beside her shook under Papa's fist and his voice roared from the other side. "You younguns come on outa there," he called, and Leeroy scampered from the room.

Enie jumped out of bed and stripped her night-gown off. She noticed, pleased, that she wasn't shivering as she pulled on her cotton drawers and flung her dress over her head. It was an old dress, faded and patched like Leeroy's overalls, and she wore it only on Saturdays, saving her three good ones for school.

Enie dabbed her freckled face with water from the bowl on the washstand. Mamma had told her last week when she had her thirteenth birthday

2

that she was too big to wash on the back porch as her brothers did, so now she had the extra chore of keeping her pitcher filled. She dared not risk inflaming Papa's temper by taking time to unplait and comb her hair, but smoothed it hastily with her damp hands on her way to the kitchen.

Papa was seated at the table, his big red hands lying on the oilcloth, a finger tapping impatiently while Mamma filled his plate at the stove. A fly explored the sticky lip of the syrup pitcher in the middle of the table, the butter was beginning to soften in its brown bowl, the blue glass toothpick-holder caught a ray of sunshine and a tiny rainbow trembled on the oilcloth beside it.

Leeroy, one eye on Papa's face, sidled onto the bench against the wall where his big brothers, T.H. and Henry Jim, were already sitting. Papa's face was mild, in spite of all the noise he'd been making, a pleased glint in the fiery blue of his eyes. Enie knew that was because of the good rain in the night. She stood beside Mamma at the stove, her hands reaching for Papa's plate.

Mamma spooned meat grease over the mountain of grits, pushed the slabs of side meat near the plate's edge. Her face was flushed; little tags of graying hair hung limp along her neck. Her motions were awkward and forced, and when she crossed the floor, things on the table jiggled.

Sue Ann, in her high chair next to Papa, talked to herself, her fat fingers folded tightly round a sodden biscuit. Her carrot-colored curls clung to her round head, her red cheeks looked hard and round as apples. Papa was all gentleness when he spoke to Sue Ann. Enie supposed he might even have spoken so to *her* once, but she couldn't remember. She thought it unlikely that Sue Ann would remember either, when she was thirteen and on the verge of being promoted to the first year in high school. For Sue Ann then, there would be fiery looks and bellowing and sometimes a raised hand, for Papa's temper matched the hair that crinkled thickly over his head and sprouted in glowing stubble from his cheeks and chin and shone red-gold along the backs of his hands and thick arms.

"Come on, girl, come on," he growled as Enie set the plate in front of him. "Haven't got all day to hold up my plowing while you moon over my vittles."

But there was a note of satisfaction under his grouchiness. He ducked his head, rumbled "Lordblessthisfoodtothegoodofourbodiesamen," and began to eat noisily. He finished, wiped his chin on the back of his hand, took his sun hat from the nail on the wall and clumped out, followed by T.H. and Henry Jim.

A peaceful silence fell upon the kitchen. Sunlight poured in at the window and winked through the knotholes behind the stove. Sue Ann sucked drowsily at her biscuit; Leeroy slid along the bench and out the door. Enie heard his rummaging in the box of odds and ends on the porch, and a moment later he trotted past the window, lugging a broken plowshare. He had made a deep hole behind the barn and for days had been working on two tunnels leading out from it. When Enie asked him where the tunnels led to, he had looked vague and said, "Far-off places." Leeroy's answer had made her wonder if he was already beginning to dream, as she did, of the world outside Tired Creek, Alabama.

Mamma lowered herself into her chair with a sigh. She crumbled a biscuit and sipped indifferently at the chicory-coffee in her cup. Enie wished the new baby would come on and get done with it, but it wasn't due till June. Mamma said it was a mighty unhandy time.

"You'll have to help me out, Enie," she'd added. Enie had helped out since she was so little she had to stand on a box to reach the dishpan, but she took the hint to mean Mamma didn't intend to hire Miss Sadie Hightower to stay the first week with this baby. Well, thirteen was old enough to take charge and it cost a dollar a day to have Miss Sadie stay.

Enie slid an extra spoonful of sugar into her coffee, since Papa wasn't around to look hard at her, and stirred it in thoughtfully. There wouldn't be much time to read, this summer, even if she got up nerve enough to ask the loan of a book from Shanes' now and then—and even less time to write down some of the things she was always making up in her head. Maybe it was just as well; her preoccupation infuriated Papa. He had disapproved of the closing of the Tired Creek school three years before, even though the new consolidated school was so much better.

"Loading all them younguns on a bus and hauling 'em to town to fill their heads full of notions, making 'em dissatisfied with what they've got." He had gone only as far as the seventh grade himself and he managed to wrestle along, didn't he? He didn't put any dependence in a lot of this folderol you heard about schools these days. Maybe you did have to make changes and the thirties weren't like before World War I, but Papa was suspicious of change—especially if it came out of books. According to him, everything had been said in one Book, and folks would do better to try to go by *it* than getting mixed up in so many notions. But Mamma had a deep respect for learning, and always glowed when Enie brought her report card home full of neat blue A's.

The sparkling, rain-washed outdoors drew Enie so she could scarcely bear the thought of making beds and sweeping floors and washing the sticky breakfast dishes. She envied the boys their plowing, could smell in imagination the new-turned earth. She could hear them yelling at the mules, Kit and Doll. To hold the moment of idleness, she asked, "When do you reckon we're going to build our new house, Mamma?"

"Oh, no telling," Mamma answered, a little too cheerfully. "Ever since the canning plant started up, things have been better for us small farmers. Long as Papa can meet his contracts with Mr. Beazely we don't have to worry about a market. Long as we're spared any bad luck." She frowned a little at Enie's silence. "Papa got the pickup, didn't he?"

Papa had got the pickup, all right. But who cared about that? Enie would never forget the day Mr. Rivers had come out from town with the brand new blue Chevrolet sedan and taken the whole Singleton family to ride in it. Up the creek and over Little Run Bridge, past the Big Washout where the Atkins shanty perched on its piling stilts on the rim of the red gully, past the yard full of little Atkinses, bug-eyed at the shiny car humming by. Out onto the highway, almost to Cedar Bluff.

"You try 'er, Clem," Mr. Rivers said when he finally turned round, and Papa took the wheel and slid the car into gear as if he'd been driving new Chevrolets all his life—instead of their balky old Ford that was nearly worn out when he bought it. But that night Papa got out his account book and did a lot of figuring, and the next week he bought the pickup truck, secondhand, from Mr. Vance.

"Where'd that Leeroy get off to?" Mamma fretted. "I wanted him to feed the biddies."

"I will." Enie got up quickly.

"Don't you stay out there mooning over them biddies," Mamma ordered sharply. "I got plenty for you to do in the house."

In the patch beyond the barnyard the dew was fast disappearing from the young collards that had missed the last frost, and on the spraddling old fig tree between the house and the lot fence tiny leaves seemed to unfold as she watched. Enie thrust the pan of food scraps through a crack and climbed nimbly over the fence instead of going down to the gate. Doc, the horse, too old for work, ambled from the far side of the lot, his nostrils twitching, and Enie reached up to pat his nose before she picked up the pan. The old horse followed her to the coop where Spot, the bantam hen, was imprisoned with her dozen children. When she had dumped the scraps into the coop, carefully keeping her fingers from Spot's beak, Enie wiped her hands on her dress and, sending a quick glance toward the house, ran to the barn. She could hear Leeroy's plow scraping and his voice talking to himself as she climbed the ladder.

The loft smelt of hay and mice and Doc, and a square of sunlight spilled in through the door that opened onto dizzy space. Enie could never look at that door without remembering the time Henry Jim had fallen through it and knocked the wind out of him. He looked blue and dead, but after T.H. shook him and pumped his arms up and down, he started to breathe and threw up his dinner where he lay.

Enie squatted before the grain basket where Tabby had put her kittens this time. There were three gray ones and an all-white one—the only white kitten Tabby had ever had. It was this one that Enie lifted from the basket, staring into its blind blue eyes before she cuddled it against her neck.

"Snowball," she crooned, "little bitty old Snowball." She had never seen snow, of course, but she knew exactly how it looked. Holding the kitten against her neck, she saw snow falling all about her—big, ragged flakes, each with a marvelously intricate design of its own, no two alike.

"Ee-eeeenie," Mamma called from the house, and Enie put the kitten back into the basket. As she backed down the ladder, the snowflakes drifting through her head melted as if the Alabama sun had touched them, and Tabby, lank and yellow-gray, slithered past her into the shadows of the barn.

Enie set the last dinner dish on the back of the shelf and closed the screenwire door of the food safe. She tiptoed to the door of Mamma's room. The cracked shades were drawn, the room stood in a still, warm twilight. Mama had just about stopped rocking, the relaxed weight of Sue Ann on her arm made her sag, lopsided.

"Can I go to the branch?" Enie whispered, and Mamma nodded, beginning to struggle up. Enie pulled her composition book from beneath the clean underwear in her bureau drawer, made sure her pencil hung from the string attached to the book, and proceeded with caution. She wasn't sure Papa had got out of sight after his dinner break, if he saw her with her writing materials he would find something for her to do.

She had reached the blackberry patch behind the lot when she saw him crossing the near field. Enie squatted down behind some dog fennel to let him get out of sight. When she was sure it was safe she got up and went hopping along over the stubble. With the weedy patch behind her and the woods stretching cool and shadowy ahead, she took her time, enjoying the whisper of pine needles and the chuckle of the stream. She left the patch and stood at the edge of the branch to watch the minnows darting about an old log that had lain in the water as long as she could remember. She and Henry Jim used to catch minnows in fruit jars. She had kept one nearly a year, once. The childishness of such a pastime brought a little sigh to her lips.

Her secret place was down beyond the curve of the branch, a little nook under a clump of willows whose drooping boughs screened her into rare and delicious privacy. A flat rock provided a place to sit, and she crawled behind the curtain of willows and curled her feet under her. Only Leeroy knew this was her sanctuary, and she had sworn him to secrecy under threat of locking him in the smokehouse should he ever tell.

It was so cool in the dense shade with the

stream's damp breath enveloping her that she shivered as she placed the composition book on her knees and touched the pencil to her tongue. For a moment she studied the column of words neatly listed inside the paper cover of the book. Some of these words she had heard her teacher use during the past year; some she had gleaned from her undirected and meager reading; some she had copied out of the dictionary she had saved up and sent to Sears Roebuck for, last fall. Slowly she read them aloud, savoring their sound as once her tongue had savored the flavor of candy. "Restraint. Crystallize. Fascination. Epitomize. Manifestation. Delectable. Inimitable." Someday she would speak words like these with ease. She practiced a lot, already, when no one was around to mock her.

On the first page began the poems she had copied from her fifth and sixth grade readers. Sometimes she read one or two aloud, thrilling to their fine swing and grandeur: *The Highwayman* and *O Captain! My Captain!*—that one always make her choke up a little. *The Duel* she knew by heart from reading it to Leeroy so many times, sharing his delight in the gingham dog and calico cat. The last one was from Shakespeare. She had copied it from this year's reader and she felt less at home with it than with the others, but it too made good reading in a sonorous voice like the preacher's, especially the first line: "The quality of mercy is not strained"; and, much more softly, "It droppeth like the gentle rain from heaven . . ." She could hear last night's gentle rain.

Today she only glanced quickly at the poems, for something was nagging in the back of her mind, urging her fingers to set it down before it was gone forever. Even so, she took time to read the excerpt from *The Ugly Duckling* on the page after the poems. " 'My, how big the world is' said all the young ones, for they undoubtedly had much more room to move about in than they had had inside their eggs. 'You don't think this is the whole world!' said their mother. 'Why, it stretches a long way on the other side of the garden, right into the parson's field.' "

With a little sigh Enie turned to a clean page and wrote her title: "From Our Back Door." As she wrote, the willow branches and the stream faded from her consciousness. She was standing on the porch at the water shelf, looking across the back yard in the early morning. She saw the blobs of shade from the fig tree and the water oak, the clean sand with tracks from the brush broom still showing, the lot fence with the broken plank T.H. kept getting out of mending, old Doc looking over the fence with sad horse wisdom in his eyes.

She had barely written the last word when the willow branches parted and Leeroy's peaked, dirt-streaked face peered through. His square brown hands were earth-caked and he smelled of sunshine and earth and little boy.

"I kilt a rattler," Leeroy announced just above a

whisper. "A big old rattler—back there in them dawg fennels. Sure nuff I did, Enie. Cross my heart and spit. I kilt him all by myself."

"What with?" Enie tried to make her voice withering but it contained a trace of interest in spite of her.

"My two hands," Leeroy cried, holding his grubby paws toward her. "I—I grabbed aholt of him right round his neck and choked him purely to death!"

"A snake hasn't got a neck," Enie said, uncurling herself.

"He has, too," Leeroy contended. "He's all neck! And I choked him till he was dead."

"Leeroy Singleton, you've just told me a great big whopping lie." It was only lately that Enie had begun to treat Leeroy this way about the tall tales he told. Till this year, even when she had known very well they were untrue, she had listened with interest to each one, never threatening or telling Mamma on him. Now she repeated harshly, "You just told a lie."

"Naw, I never . . ."

Enie fixed cold eyes on the peaked little face. "Nobody ever choked a rattlesnake and you know it."

"I did," Leeroy insisted, but some of the swagger had gone out of him. He pinched a leaf from a limb, stuck it to his tongue.

"All right then, show me," Enie challenged. To her surprise Leeroy turned and made off up the path, looking back to see if she followed. At the patch, in a thick clump of dog fennel, he stopped and pointed. His eyes were bright and Enie looked sharply along the ground. "See him?" Leeroy crowed. "Old dead snake. Dead as a doornail."

"There is no rattler there, Leeroy. Not even a little old chicken snake. What makes you say things are so when they're not at all? Folks'll get to thinking you're tetched in your head."

Leeroy squatted and stared at the grass in delighted horror. His shoulder blades stood up under his old plaid shirt. Enie turned and walked away, leaving him alone with his rattler.

2

EVERY FOURTH SUNDAY Brother Dix came from town and preached at the Pleasant Grove Baptist Church. Mamma didn't go this Sunday; she had got so big, the hard benches hurt her back and the three-mile ride in the pickup truck was too rough for her.

"Me and Sue Ann will just have us a nice time by ourselves," she said, twitching at the hem of Enie's flowered dimity. The dress was too short, like all her last summer's dresses, and tight across the chest. The style was childish, too, Enie thought, and she felt long-legged and gawky as a colt. Her patent leather slippers were short, too, and cramped her toes. But it was worth the discomfort to be able to look down and see them still shiny, with just a little crack across the toes that scarcely showed. Her rayon stockings itched her legs because she wasn't used to stockings. She scowled at the face in the looking glass, convinced that at least a dozen big, brown freckles had erupted across her forehead since last preaching Sunday.

Papa hollered at her from the front yard where he was walking up and down under the chinaberry tree, and she grabbed her hat from the bed and hurried out. Papa was gingerly feeling his face where he had shaved too close; his hair was damp and plastered so close to his head that the thick waves were only faint crinkles. He looked too big for his blue serge suit, and the black felt hat he set firmly upon his head as Enie approached made him taller than ever. His lips worried the frayed toothpick between them as if determined to extract the last bit of good from it before he spat it out.

Enie sat up in the cab with Papa and T.H., and Henry Jim and Leeroy rode in the back. T.H. looked nearly as uncomfortable as Papa in his Sunday clothes. His big-knuckled hands looked ashamed, hanging below his coat sleeves, and the pimples on his brooding face stood out angry and inflamed. He was sixteen years old and as tall as Papa, though his immature body was still thin as a reed and his narrow shoulders rounded from field work. Lately Enie couldn't help feeling sorry for him. He looked so unhappy most of the time. She knew he hated Papa's bossing him around and making him work all the time, never letting him hang around the streets in Green Pine like the Vance and Hightower boys did.

Henry Jim was nothing like T.H. He was only a year younger but there was still a lot of little boy in him. His teasing was of the merry, harmless sort, and he was stocky and round-faced with slightly squinting blue eyes and hair more sandy than red. As aggravating as Enie frequently found him, she had to admit he had none of the meanness that ran in a dark streak through T.H. He didn't seem to mind jolting along in the back of the truck with Leeroy, the dust powdering their Sunday pants.

Papa darted sharp looks at the fields on either side of the road: Vance's. Shane's. Elkins'. Hightower's. Shane's again—a little better, the soil darker, richer looking. Papa chewed his lips and Enie could tell that the sight of Mr. Tom Shane's fields stirred a feeling in him that wasn't fit to take to preaching. She could fairly see him thinking, That Tom Shane. Always ahead. Always top dog. "Vances have gone," he observed aloud as they passed the comfortable-looking house with the big pecan grove on one side. "Will Vance never shut a carhouse door in his life."

The Elkins place was next—a neat white house with green trim. Enie knew that, like Vance's, it was equipped with running water, electricity and a telephone. Not to mention the radio and the washing machine. Enie ached with envy, at times, of these more prosperous neighbors, but once, when she revealed it in a muttered comment, Mamma said, "Now, Earline, don't you go fretting yourself over what folks have that money can buy."

In the strip of woods beyond the Elkins place bay trees were in bloom, and here and there a dogwood's white-starred branches showed like a lace petticoat. The trees in Mr. Jimmy Hightower's peach orchard were pink with blossom, and the old rail fence that surrounded the Howells' corn patch sagged under honeysuckle. The truck was beginning to heat up by the time the Shane house showed bits of white through the trees around it.

Mr. Tom Shane was said to be the richest farmer in Covington County, Alabama. A porch with fluted columns ran the width of the tall house; green blinds flanked the windows; the chimneys rose, proud and haughty, above the treetops; and a half acre of ground spread in arrogant waste from the brick steps to the crepe myrtle hedge that separated it from the road. A long, straight lane bordered with poplars led from the road through the porte-cochere, back to the garage and stable and other outbuildings.

The Shanes would not be at Pleasant Grove Church. They were the only Catholic family for miles around, and had to drive all the way to Cedar Bluff to church. Papa held the Shanes' religion against them, rumbling darkly about "them that bow down to idols of wood and stone," but Enie found everything to do with the Shanes interesting. Once, when Papa made a scoffing remark about Mr. Tom Shane's farming "out of books,"

Enie hadn't been able to stop herself saying that it worked—wasn't he the richest farmer in Covington County?

Papa had replied witheringly that luck and greed had made Shane's circumstances what they were today. "He's a land hawg," Papa said, "an' he's chock full of the luck of the Irish you hear tell of. Let alone the land that was left to him, clear and free, just like his will be left to his younguns whether they ever turn a hand or not. Back when cotton was kind in these parts, Tom Shane's pa made a fortune. Any man can add to a fortune. It's startin' from scratch that takes doing."

But Enie went right on thinking that book learning had played a considerable part in Mr. Tom's success.

The road twisted off to the left, narrower and sandier, and the water in the radiator began to boil. Miss Katy Powell's store squatted at the bend of the road, presenting a closed Sunday face, its red gasoline pump at one side, a wisp of smoke rising palely from the little chimney at the back where Miss Katy lived. A quarter of a mile beyond was Pleasant Grove Church.

Papa brought the truck to a panting stop under a sycamore tree, cautioned the children in his stern before-preaching voice to behave themselves or they knew what they'd get when they got home, and T.H. scowlingly unwound the baling wire from the broken door-catch. Enie's dress flew up, showing the crocheted edge of her Sunday petticoat as she jumped off the high running board.

The grove was spotted with people, dignified in their Sunday clothes and with manners to match them. Men squatted, country fashion, on their heels, their dark hats pulled low on their foreheads; children played without boisterousness about the nakedly protruding roots of the great oak trees. Perhaps a dozen cars and half as many pickup trucks stood about the edge of the grove, and the Jasons' mule Daniel hung his aging head and switched at flies as he stood patiently between the shafts of the old-fashioned buggy. Every family in Tired Creek was represented at church except the Shanes. Even a few Atkinses drifted about the churchyard, their garments and faces fairly clean.

Lou Addie Jason stood on the top step of the white frame church building. She was a thin little girl with brown hair lying meekly on her shoulders. Her pink lips were always parted a little and her skin had a bluish transparency Enie thought was beautiful, but when she laughed, Lou Addie always put her hand over her mouth to hide the discolored tooth whose nerve had died. She came slowly toward the Singletons now with a soft, "Hey, Enie."

"Hey, Lou Addie. Did you get the rest of the examples?" Arithmetic was a bugbear to Lou Addie, and all year Enie had been dragging her through the assignments.

Lou Addie nodded with a little snuffle. "Ote helped me with the last two long ones you didn't have time to do." She slipped a toothpick arm through Enie's. "Let's sit together, hear?"

"Okay. I got to keep Leeroy with me, though. He's liable to cut up, with Papa in the choir. Do you want to go in now?"

The interior of the church was pleasantly cool, though the rough wooden benches had already been supplied with cardboard fans from Williams' Pharmacy in Green Pine. Printed on them in large black letters were some of the items that could be bought at the drugstore, and in smaller letters at the bottom, a verse of scripture—"Come unto me all ye that labour and are heavy laden and I will give ye rest."

Enie, Leeroy and Lou Addie traipsed down the uncarpeted aisle and slid onto the bench occupied by Mrs. Vance and her daughter Carol. Brother Dix had not arrived, but the atmosphere was one of respect and gentle awe, its quiet broken only by the occasional cry of a baby in its mother's arms or the scrape of feet on the bare floor. No whispering, no giggling, an air of waiting, of expectation.

A group of boys T.H.'s age clattered into the church and crowded onto a bench near the back, scraping their great feet and creaking the bench, then slowly settling to quiet. Papa and the other singers marched importantly up front and took the two benches facing the congregation. Leaving them, Enie's eyes found the table with the white cloth humped over the pitcher of grape juice and covering the plates of light bread cut into neat cubes.

Enie could not take communion because she did not belong to the church. Last year, during the revival, she had almost joined. Her heart had pounded and tears had run down her face while the choir implored, *"Why* not now? *Why* not now?" It was just as if Brother Dix and all the saved were looking through her skin at all the tucked-away sins she did not even allow herself to look at when she could help it. But she wasn't ready to be a church member like those who had taken their place on the side of the Lord, as Brother Dix said, and been baptized in the creek after the revival. She supposed she would have to join sometime. But not yet, not just yet.

Miss Katy Powell whisked past Enie, her small, sharp face lifted, the flat black straw hat she had worn to church ever since Enie could remember, in season and out, set firmly on her head.

The last stragglers had come in from the grove and the church was filled when Brother Dix arrived. Watching him walk swiftly toward the rostrum, his Bible in his long, thin hand, Enie thought of all the fried chicken he had consumed the last time he'd had dinner with them. He had finished up with two ample slices of lemon-cheese cake, too, but no matter how much he ate he never got any fatter. He was long and thin all over—thin as a scantling and so tall he stooped a little, as if he might be about to hit his head on something any minute.

Brother Dix announced the hymn number and read the first verse out to the congregation before Miss Elsie Mae Howells played a few crashing chords on the piano that was still new and a joy to listen to after the wheezing old organ that had spoilt the singing for years. Even Papa, who generally balked at new proposals on principle—especially if they involved the spending of money—had contributed three dollars toward the purchase of the piano.

Miss Elsie Mae played like Papa sang, putting her whole soul into it. She banged down purposefully on the bass and threw little curlicues into the treble till Mamma said it didn't hardly seem proper for sacred music. Papa's strong bass rolled out like thunder in the little church, and all the other singers did their best to keep up with him.

The sermon was not as long as usual because time had to be saved for the Lord's Supper. While they were singing the hymn at the end of the sermon, Enie took Leeroy by the hand and, though he pulled back and made a face at her, led him out of the church.

"It ain't over yet," Leeroy protested in a loud voice as they reached the door. Enie shook him, not letting go of his hand till they were outside.

"We can't partake," she said.

"Why?" Leeroy whined, kicking sand over Enie's slippers.

"We're not members," Enie said. She stooped to wipe her slippers with her handkerchief, hoping her brief answer would satisfy him. She didn't feel she understood well enough herself to explain the symbolism of the bread and grape juice so Leeroy could grasp it, let alone the state of grace one must have in order to participate.

Leeroy wandered toward the Jasons' mule and Enie called him back. Mr. Thaddy Atkins had been kicked by a mule when he was a boy, and had a silver plate inside his skull to this very day, Enie had heard tell, and Mamma said maybe that was what made him so no-account he wouldn't work. Enie wondered how it felt to have a silver plate in your head. When she was little she thought it was like the plates they passed the bread in for communion at Church—round and beaded round the edge. Though she had long known better than that, it was awful to think of a piece of metal—even precious metal—between brain and bone and skin.

"Let's go in the graveyard," she suggested, and Leeroy's look of boredom vanished. He trotted happily round to the back of the church with her. They let themselves in at the wire gate and walked aimlessly about, careful not to step on the graves. Leeroy called from a corner of the graveyard that he'd found a gopher hole, and Enie went over to look at it.

"My sore hurts," Leeroy complained. "It's my shoes hurts it."

"You can't take 'em off. Not till you get home."

Leeroy sat down on a gravestone. "I want to," he insisted, tugging at the shoe. "I'm agoin' to."

"You can't. And get up off of that grave, Leeroy."

"How come?"

"It don't show respect. Look here, Leeroy! Here's a marble." She stooped and dug the partially buried marble from the sand. "It's a real pretty out. Leeroy's face shone.

"A glassy! Kin I have it! I ain't got any but peewees."

Enie hesitated, thinking of the spool box she had at home in the dresser drawer beneath her underwear. It was half full of bits of colored glass she had collected through the years. What on earth would a teen-age girl want with a marble—even a blue one with a dark-red swirl in the center? She watched Leeroy's hands cradling it, holding it against his cheek, and felt something dissolve inside her. It was true he had only the clay ones, five for a penny . . .

"I reckon you can have it."

They wandered about a little more. Suddenly Leeroy stiffened. "I seen a fox," he whispered. Enie looked past his rigidly pointing finger—and of course there was only the sagging fence covered with Dorothy Perkins rose vines. Leeroy had told a lie in the very shadow of the church on preaching Sunday with the Lord's Supper being served inside. She would have to tell on Leeroy; there was no getting around it any longer. Without meaning to, she asked, "What did he look like?"

"Like—like a fox," Leeroy said.

"How big was he?"

"Bigger'n you an me put together." He was beginning to tremble.

"You never saw any fox, Leeroy," Enie said patiently. "I don't believe there's any foxes around Tired Creek atall. If there was, they wouldn't show theirselves in broad day."

"This here one did," Leeroy insisted. "I seen him."

"We better tell Papa about it, then, so he can get his gun and come after him. He'll be eating our chickens."

Leeroy put the marble in his mouth and sucked on it. "Maybe," he said, squeezing his eyes into slits, "I jest *thought* I seen him. Maybe he was a feist dawg—or somepin. I don't see no use aworryin' Papa. Do you, Enie, huh?"

The anxiety in his tone touched Enie. He looked so little; she wanted to take his hand, to give him now and forever her protection and loyalty. But she distrusted the tenderness Leeroy could uncover in her. To admit it would leave her defenseless before him.

"They're singing the last song now," she said. "We better go wait in the pickup."

Watching the people come slowly out of the church, Enie felt faintly inferior to the girls who were members. All of a sudden Carol and Lou Addie seemed more adult than she; Enie felt awkward and childish, standing beside the truck with Leeroy. Well, there wasn't anything she could do about it. Mamma had said she would know when she had "an experience of grace;" until she had it, she wouldn't be saved and she would just have to wait for it.

Papa was talking to Miss Elsie Mae Howells on the church steps. About the music, Enie supposed, though Miss Elsie Mae was not one to hold back when there was a man around to talk to and giggle at. Enie thought Miss Elsie Mae must be awfully old—thirty-five, or forty, maybe—but she acted like a girl in her teens when she was around the men. Folks said she had been engaged to a fellow in Montgomery County, years ago, and he had jilted her and married another girl. They said that for a long time she wouldn't look at or speak to any male creature, treated them all like dirt. Then when she was old enough to know better, the married women around Tired Creek said, she had started acting like a fool. Enie wished Papa would break away; her feet hurt and Leeroy was whining and pestering her.

They were all in the pickup at last. The ride home gave Enie more pleasure than the trip to church—maybe because the sermon was over and her cramped feet out of the pinching slippers. The sun was still high and bright, and the scent of honeysuckle was sweet in the air. Papa's rested

Sunday mood kindly enveloped her—he didn't even seem to be thinking of Mr. Tom Shane's fields but looked amiably ahead of him at the road. The preacher whizzed by, honked the horn of his shiny Ford, and Papa honked back. The world seemed sweet and bright and swelling with summer promise. Enie wriggled her toes and leaned back, feeling drowsy and quiet inside.

3

THE SATURDAY after school was out Enie heard Mamma tell Papa to go on to town—she needed groceries and something was wrong with the pickup that T.H. couldn't fix; they'd have to take it to the garage and let Mr. Kelly have a look at it. Mamma said she didn't know as she felt any different from what she had for the last week—and that was like she couldn't heft herself out of her chair if somebody was to hold a gun on her. So Papa and T.H. drove off after chores with the truck motor coughing and knocking, and Mamma said worriedly she hoped they would make it to the garage all right.

Enie washed up the milk things and breakfast dishes, made all the beds and swept the floors, stopping every now and then to stare into space and remind herself she had completed all the elementary grades and would be a high school student when next the yellow bus conveyed her to Green Pine school. For more than a year, it seemed to Enie, she had been on the lookout for a turning point of some sort, a moment in her life she would recognize as such; surely it would come with the beginning of high school. Four years— only four more precious years—then what? College, that was what.

Nobody knew yet but Enie herself, but her mind was made up; somehow or other she would manage to acquire enough education for a teacher's certificate. Nothing could hold her in Tired Creek then, nothing.

"I'm going to hit that big new highway and go," she muttered, tingling as she sent her broom in vigorous strokes across the porch. "I'm going up north and see snow, I'm going to see the ocean— and a mountain, a real mountain, so high you can look down into clouds from the top of it. And— maybe—before I do that, I'll read a thousand books."

She put her broom away and came back to sit on the edge of the porch and dream into the yard. She looked at the dark green bottles Mamma had partially buried in two straight rows, one on either side of the sandy walk. The bottles' necks were underground, their bottoms above and almost overlapping so that they made a bright edging and winked in the dappled sunshine the oak tree allowed them. Enie intended to have a gold ring with an emerald to gleam like the bottles on that Someday that grew in importance each year of her life. The swing hung from a branch of the oak as big around as Sue Ann; when nobody was there to think her childish, Enie still loved to stand with her bare feet firmly planted on the board, worn smooth by little Singletons' bottoms, and pump to a delirious height, her skirts and pigtails flying, her mind flying beyond her body toward the bright infinity toward which it thrust tentative feelers. The prince's-feather over in the fence corner was a deep cerise; Enie meant to have a velvet cape, shirred on the shoulders, to wear over the sweeping gowns Someday's formal occasions would demand.

She drew the end of a pigtail across her chin, then tossed it back over her shoulder. The chinaberry leaves hung still; Minnie, the dog, scratched, whined, and crawled under the step as if it were midsummer. Lecroy and Sue Ann played, sweet as angels, under the chinaberry tree. Enie was just about to go in for her composition book when Mamma called from the front room.

"I spect you better keep the fire up," she said, and Enie saw she looked hollowed-eyed, changed in the last hour.

"Why, Mamma? It's so hot—I thought you said we'd have buttermilk and bread for dinner."

"I know. It's hot and I said that, but you do like I say, now. Keep up the fire."

Enie knew, then. It was beginning. With Papa

off in town with the truck. No way to get the doctor or Miss Sadie Hightower.

She poked a stick of wood into the stove and hurried back to the front room. The instructions Mamma had given her a week ago raced through her mind. She was to get Papa—but Papa was five miles away in Green Pine; so was T.H., and Henry Jim was clean out of sight in the onion patch. She was to take Leeroy and Sue Ann to Mrs. Vance's and telephone the doctor from there. But she couldn't leave Mamma alone at the house with a baby coming!

"I've had two pains," Mamma said as calmly as she would say the weather was unseasonably hot. "It'll be a spell, no need to worry."

Enie stood beside the bed, feeling ignorance overwhelm her.

"Papa likely won't be back here before two-three o'clock this afternoon," Mamma was saying. "You find Henry Jim and get him to take the little ones to Vances'. Listen to me close, Enie. Tell Henry Jim to ask Mrs. Vance to get word to Sadie Hightower, then phone Dr. Helms—we'll pay her back the cost of the calls." Mamma wiped her face with one of Papa's Sunday handkerchiefs. "You got it straight?"

"Yessum." Enie tried to match Mamma's calm but her heart was jumping like a rabbit's.

"Be sure you get your hat, and bring me the clock first. I don't want to hurry the pains by stirring round any more'n I purely have to."

Enie got the clock off the shelf over the stove. It had a crack across its face, so you had to look at it carefully to tell the time. She set it on the bureau so Mamma could see it and took off across the yard, through the patch of millet Mamma grew for chicken feed, and across the fields, not bothering to land her feet carefully between the rows, plunging along any old way. She was out of breath and there was a pain needling her side when she saw Henry Jim's straw-hatted head. He turned, his hands slowly falling from the handles of the cultivator.

"It's the baby," Enie panted. "You got to hurry. Get up to the house and take the kids to Vances'." She rattled off Mamma's instructions as fast as she could, and Henry Jim stared at her as if he hadn't heard a word, so she had to go through it again. "You're obliged to *hurry*, Henry Jim, you hear me?"

Henry Jim began to lope across the rows, Enie following as fast as the stitch in her side would let her. When she got to the house, he was already setting off down the road toward Vances', pulling Sue Ann in Leeroy's old wagon. Leeroy trotted alongside, his unanswered questions rising above the squeak of the wagon wheels. Enie hung her hat on its nail and went to the front room. Mamma was lying back with her eyes closed. The clock ticked heartlessly, its hands pointing to half-past ten. Without opening her eyes, Mamma said, "Better put some wood in the stove, honey, and fill the kettle."

In her clumsy haste Enie ran a sliver into her hand as she pushed the stick of pine into the stove. She lifted the lid of the iron kettle, saw it was half full, filled it from the bucket and dragged it forward to the hottest part of the stove. She began to pray agitatedly—Let everything be all right. Let me do everything like I ought to. Let Miz Sade get here in time.

There was no use fighting fear any longer. What if the baby came before anybody got here? If only Papa hadn't gone to town . . . If only he would come, now, this minute! She could forgive him the grudges of a lifetime if only he would come and get her out of this predicament.

She went in to Mamma, pulled the rocker up to the bed and sat down. "What does it feel like, Mamma?" If they could keep talking, maybe it wouldn't seem so long before somebody came.

"I can't tell you, honey. You'll know someday— when your turn comes. What time does it say now?"

"Ten minutes till eleven." Enie was out of her chair, her fingers twisting. "I'll go see if anybody's coming up the road." She hung over the gate and looked down the road toward Vances', then up the road toward town. She shaded her eyes with her hand and looked till her eyeballs stung. Not a car, not a beast, not a human was in sight. She went slowly back to the house.

Laying Mamma's clean nightgown on the bed, Enie refused to look at the clock. Why hadn't Miz Sade got here? What had happened to Henry Jim? It was a long walk, of course, and heavy going through the sand with the wagon . . .

"Let me help you, Mamma." She drew the damp dress from Mamma's shoulders, shook out the nightgown she had ironed just yesterday. She wished her heart would slow down a little; it made her sick at her stomach, beating so fast. This was worse than the time she and Henry Jim got lost in the woods back of Shanes' and thought they would have to spend the night wandering and calling. It was worse than anything she could remember.

When Leeroy was born Enie had spent an enchanted afternoon at Miss Katy's store, and when Sue Ann gave signs of putting in her appearance Enie had merely had to take Leeroy to Vances'. Mr. Vance had brought them home in his truck when it was all over and Mamma peacefully asleep.

Enie folded the counterpane over the foot of the bed, laid the sheet back, smoothed the bottom one, hearing the length of oilcloth crackle under her trembling hands. She ran to put wood in the stove, brought a cup of tepid water which Mamma drank greedily, spilling a little on her clean gown. The clock said eleven-thirty.

She couldn't believe it when she heard the car, thought it was a part of the craziness that was going to send her screaming down the road for help. But as she stepped into the hall, the cup of water still in her hands, flesh-and-blood steps crossed the porch, the screen door with the patch in the middle opened and slapped shut, and Miss Sadie Hightower's tall, spare shape appeared, beautiful beyond compare. Behind her stood Henry Jim, fiddling with the frayed brim of his sun hat. The cup hit the floor with a crash, and Enie went down on her knees to pick the pieces of crockery out of the spreading puddle.

"Well, mercy me! Look at you, breaking your ma's dishes." Miz Sade stepped into the front room. "Doc'll be here any minute," she threw over her shoulder at Enie. She set her worn bag on a chair and opened it.

"Ain't it a scorcher for so early in the year! You picked a day for such a chore, Elnora." She winked at Mamma who had just had a pain and was panting weakly in a pool of sweat. "Now, if you'll do a disappearin' act, honey, I'll have a look at your mamma and see how we're doing."

Henry Jim was lying on the back porch in the shade. He had poured a bucket of water over his head and was indisposed to talk, but Enie dragged out of him what had happened. When he found nobody home at Vances'—it being Saturday, they had all gone to town, of course—he had gone on to the Elkins' house. He'd left the kids with Mrs. Elkins and gone on to Hightowers' as fast as he could. Miz Sade hadn't taken a minute getting ready, but when she went to back her car out of the barn, there was a flat tire and Henry Jim and Mr. Jimmy had it to fix.

"Miz Sade got Mr. Jimmy out of the field by ringing the dinner bell like the house was afire," Henry Jim recalled, grinning broadly, "and I'm tellin' you he sure come acallihootin'." While the tire was being changed Miz Sade called Dr. Helms —had to try three or four places before she got him rounded up. "Lordy mercy, I'm tired," Henry Jim finished, stretching his legs. "Hungry, too."

Enie pulled herself up from the step. "I'll fix you some dinner." She hadn't once thought of food, didn't want a bite now. Dr. Helms came while Enie was frying side meat and hoecake for Henry Jim, and the last lingering shred of her fear dissolved at the sound of his big voice. Mamma would be all right now. She set a heaped plate in front of Henry Jim and tilted the coffeepot to pour herself a cup when the thin, high wail floated out from the front room. Henry Jim looked startled, then grinned foolishly at Enie. He said not a word, just went on eating, looking very much like Papa.

"It's come," Enie said dazedly. "The new baby's come."

Henry Jim wiped his mouth on his sleeve and went to join his cultivator in the onion patch. Enie knew he had had his fill of the house and women. She was sipping her coffee when Miz Sade sailed into the kitchen, wet with perspiration and beaming with triumph.

"Well, girl we've gone and done it again.

There's a new sister for you to tote around and get more hump-shouldered than you are already. You better remember to hold up your chest or the boys won't look at you. Coffee in that pot? Doc'll be wanting some in a little bit." She pulled the kettle forward to pour water into the wash pan she carried. "Pretty a little girl as I ever helped fetch," she said, "but then your mamma always has pretty babies. Soon's I get them fixed up and comfy, you come along and look at her."

But Enie was not in any hurry. She sat in the grateful quiet of the hot kitchen, the morning's terror already dimming, taking on a welcome unreality. It had turned out all right, after all. Just the same, Enie felt that she had aged a great deal in the past few hours—and she had made up her mind about one thing: she wasn't going to have any babies, ever.

Dr. Helms's car had hardly got out of sight when the pickup rattled to a stop behind Miz Sade's car. T.H. began getting the groceries out, but Papa stomped onto the porch looking as if somebody had put something over on him.

"About time," Enie heard Miz Sade josh him. "Look who's come looking for a place to live while you was gallivantin' round town!"

From the hall, Enie watched Papa go over to the bed. She saw him look down, saw Mamma's white face crinkle in a smile. An obscure resentment twitched at Enie as she move toward the kitchen.

The dishes wouldn't wash themselves, she reasoned, knowing suddenly that she was bone-tired, and this summer there would be twice as many diapers.

4

THAT WAS a strange summer.

Some days Enie felt as sober and tired as an old woman, lugging and changing babies, sweeping yards, helping Mamma with the preserving in a kitchen that was like an oven before nine in the morning. Other times she wanted to run and yell and climb trees like a kid. When Mamma kept her busy with chores, she itched to write; but when she had an hour to herself she couldn't think of a word.

She would sit staring through the willow screen, slap morosely at mosquitoes, ache with longing to go far away from Tired Creek to some place she had never seen. These were the times when the fear of being stuck here for life rose like a fever in her.

And always, now, everything was Papa's fault.

She supposed she had never loved him—Papa wasn't the kind of person you loved, somehow—but it was this summer, this queer summer she was thirteen, that she began to hate him. It was a dreadful worry, this sin on her soul. She would push the feeling down again and again, but it always came rushing and boiling up when Papa yelled at her for "mooning," or made Leeroy cry, or whipped Henry Jim for neglecting a chore. She felt, all that summer, as if she were crawling with sin. Mamma noticed that there was something wrong with her and threatened to make up a mess of the tonic she believed in so firmly. She said Enie was outgrowing her strength and couldn't keep up with herself, much less with all the work there was to do. Thinking to please her, Mamma said Enie could name the new baby.

Enie didn't have to think long about that. There were a dozen or more lovely, romantic, fanciful names she used in the stories she was always making up about places where it snowed and people lived excitingly. Almost absentmindedly she picked Jennifer. Papa grunted when he heard it and never called the baby anything but Jenny. The others picked it up, of course, and laughed at Enie into the bargain when she called such a little nubbin a long, fancy name, and quite soon, she, too, gave up and said Jenny along with the rest.

Mr. Tom Shane came on a hot July afternoon while Papa was taking his after-dinner break, stretched full length on a quilt on the porch. He sat up slowly, his chest hair showing golden where his sweaty shirt lay open. From the swing under the oak Enie watched Mr. Shane get out of his car, come through the gate and pass unhurriedly down the walk between the green bottles. His seersucker suit was wrinkled and not very clean, his old panama hat was limp and yellow. He had a broad, lean face and a beaklike nose, and his eyes had yellow specks in them.

"Evenin', Clem," Mr. Shane said, and Papa replied, "Evenin'."

Enie knew Mr. Shane had come to talk to Papa about the west field; he'd been trying to buy that bit of land a long time, but Papa wouldn't sell. Besides not wanting to part with any of his land, Papa seemed to derive a curious satisfaction out of thwarting Mr. Tom Shane. Even four years ago, when times were so hard folks were wondering how they were going to keep on eating, Papa had turned Mr. Shane down flat. Still, Mr. Tom wouldn't give up. He kept coming back at Papa. determined to get that field.

Enie ran Sue Ann down in the corner of the yard, under the prince's-feather, and carried her, shrieking, round the house and in the back door. Mamma was standing at the front room window, looking out at Papa and Mr. Shane. She turned as

Enie came in and picked up the shirt she had been patching.

"See can you get Sue Ann off to sleep," she suggested, and Enie dragged the rocker up near the window and coaxed Sue Ann to her lap. The men's voices rumbled steadily on the other side of the window, the rocker squeaked rhythmically, Sue Ann stopped squirming and sagged, hot and heavy, on Enie's arm, and Enie's thoughts hovered round the Shanes whose doings were like bright threads woven into the fabric of her life.

Mr. Tom Shane had once given her a lift to Miss Katy Powell's store, and she had been so shy she could barely get out "yes, sir" and "no, sir" in answer to the soft-spoken questions he put to her. He had called Enie his "little friend" whenever they met after that—until the last year or so when she'd run up so tall.

And there was the time Mamma sent Enie and Henry Jim to pick blackberries, and Rowan Shane slipped out of her yard and joined them. They had played in the creek, and Enie and Henry Jim got whippings when they got home at dusk-dark with their lard buckets only half full of berries. Some time after that, Enie was passing the Shanes' on an errand, and Rowan called to her from the other side of the myrtle hedge. "Mamma's been to Montgomery," she said when Enie was in the yard with her, "to buy new things for me to take away to school. Want to see them?"

The house was cool and shadowy after the Sep-

tember glare outdoors and so big that Enie felt like
an animated doll padding soundlessly on her dusty
bare feet along the darkly shining floor of the wide
hall. When she followed Rowan up the curving
stairway she wished she had a dozen eyes so she
wouldn't miss anything. In Rowan's room she had
felt paralyzed by the pink-and-white fairy-tale
prettiness. Rowan was just a little girl, but this was
her very own room. She didn't have to share the
white bed or the beautiful dresser, though it had
three shining mirrors all hinged together and a
little bench to sit on and see yourself reflected three
times over.

And the clothes! Enie would never forget those
clothes. The bed was covered with boxes, and
tissue paper lay scattered on the floor with its thick
carpet into which her bare toes sank deliciously.
There must have been a dozen dresses; there were
stacks of thin, white underwear, and—finally—on
a hanger in the white wardrobe whose doors
Rowan proudly flung open, a dear little dark blue
coat with a white collar starched stiff as a board.
Rowan climbed on a chair and took from the shelf
of the wardrobe a little round scarlet hat and a red
velvet purse.

"At the school," Rowan explained, making a
face that brought laughter bubbling up in Enie,
awed through she was, "I'll have to wear a uniform. A horrid, ugly old thing. Long black stockings, too. These"—she waved a hand toward the

hangers—"are for when I go visiting our relatives in Mobile."

Enie was a child then, happy in the life she led, knowing nothing else. But that little glimpse had made her aware that there were other ways of living and that the Shanes were not like other folks in Tired Creek. It was the end of any sort of intimacy between Enie and Rowan Shane. After she went away, Rowan always seemed more than the two years older than Enie, and their lives never touched at any point. But the memory stayed bright and alive through the years.

The next memory was not a bright one, but just as much alive as the others. Enie had tried to forget it, but it kept popping up, filling her with a kind of excitement that was half-fear, and that always left her feeling strangely guilty and regretful and confused. As she grew older, the confusion was gradually clarified by knowledge. But the fear and the guilt—and the bewildering excitement—remained.

It happened four summers ago when Enie was nine years old.

She was looking for a guinea hen's nest, this side of Shane's cane field. Poking around in the weeds close to a great clump of honeysuckle that had taken the fence between Singleton's and Shanes' land, she had heard a faint rustling. Thinking it might be the guinea hen, she had sneaked right up to the thicket and peeped round the end of it. In the little tunnel inside that was dim and secret and sweet-smelling her unbelieving eyes made out two human forms. Side by side, closer than close, arms entwined, faces a mingled blur in the dimness. Enie hastily drew back from the entrance of the thicket as she recognized Bliss Atkins and Ralph Shane under the vines.

Forgetting her errand, Enie fled across the stubbly field. When, later, she considered what she had seen, she felt a mixture of emotions that she could not understand. She was no less wise than other farm children for whom the mating of beasts was as much a part of day-to-day experience as rain, sun, frost or autumn wind, as the planting of seed and the rampant growth in summer. But she had never thought of a boy and a girl together in such secrecy and nearness. She knew, even in the frantic moments of flight, that she would never tell a living soul, and there was a loneliness in the secret she had not sought to know.

In the time that followed, Enie felt a grief and a guilt for Ralph—because he was a Shane and Rowan's brother. All her life she had heard the Atkinses referred to as "trash," and quickly piecing together fragments of adult remarks about Bliss, she understood with a child's quickness that this was part of what was meant by "trash." Bliss wasn't very smart; she had quit school because she couldn't keep up with the other pupils in Tired Creek. But Ralph was smarter than any of the others; Mamma said that was why Mr. Tom Shane took him to Green Pine every day to school before consolidation and the bus; not, as some folks said, that Mrs. Shane thought her boy was too good to go to school with the neighbors' kids. Ralph should not have been with Bliss Atkins under the honeysuckle.

It seemed a long time afterward that Mrs. Vance was spending the afternoon with Mamma, picking over figs on the porch, preparing them for canning. Enie was minding Leeroy, who was the baby then, when Mrs. Vance's voice, suddenly hushed and greedy, caught her attention. She bent over the words she was spelling out with a twig in the sand but listened intently. Mrs. Vance told Mamma a boy had got Bliss Atkins in trouble.

"They say she give the Shane boy's name. Only, how can they prove anything, way she's been carryin' on since she quit school? Them Atkinses are trash, Elnora, just purentee trash!"

"Why, that boy's no more than a child hisself," Mamma answered, shocked and sad. "He's not more'n seventeen." Mamma seemed to notice Enie listening then and told her to go help Henry Jim tote in his wood, and she hadn't heard any more. Then or ever.

Ralph Shane went away to school, after that. He had always been a quiet, bookish boy and his absence made little difference to the community. He had been stricken with infantile paralysis when he was a baby and his right foot dragged a little. Papa said he would never make a farmer but reckoned he wouldn't have, anyhow, with his face shoved in a book half the time.

The talk died down, as talk always must; as the baby born too soon had died.

Last summer Bliss Atkins had run off with a drummer that hung around the hotel in Green Pine, and Ralph Shane was at home again. He had finished college, they said, and no longer looked like the quiet, bookish boy Enie remembered. He was a man grown now, tall and wide-shouldered, but his foot still dragged when he walked and he was still fair-haired like his sister Rowan. He rode on a bay mare named Sweet Lou, and in spite of Papa's predictions helped his father run the place. Enie wondered if he remembered as clearly as she did, the little room under the honeysuckle. He had traveled a long way from it in four years.

The rocking chair squeaked to a stop and Enie shifted Sue Ann's sticky weight to ease the arm that had gone to sleep. Mr. Shane was going down the walk and Papa was standing on the step in his bare feet, watching him go. The four years had done things for Enie, too, she thought, pushing Sue Ann's mop of curls away from the forehead that was finely peppered with heat rash. She knew all about boys getting girls in trouble now, of course—knew long before Mamma talked to her last winter and told her that what was happening to Enie happens to all girls.

Papa came through the house as Enie was putting Sue Ann on the cot. He had pulled his shoes

on and his steps were loud and angry. He went
back to the water shelf and Enie heard the clank
of the tin dipper against the side of the bucket,
then Papa's voice ranting to Mamma. "Takes a
Shane to think that when a man's down on his luck
he'll make hisself worse off by gettin' rid of the
little he's got."

"You're not so down on your luck, Clement.
Not now," Mamma answered, firmly. "We got
plenty to eat and a good shelter over our heads.
Times are better by a heap than a while back."

"Well, I'm not about to sell ary foot of my land
to no Shane—and he might just as well get it
through his bull head! I can hold out just as . . ."

Enie didn't listen to any more. She'd been hearing it all her life, it seemed. It was true, she
couldn't see what Mr. Tom Shane wanted with
more land—but that was his business. After Papa
had gone to the field, she went to Mamma and
asked point-blank: "What makes Papa hate Mr.
Tom Shane so?"

Mamma folded the shirt she had repaired and
laid it in the dresser drawer. "He don't *hate* Mr.
Tom, Enie. It's hard on him seein' anybody have
so much, I reckon, when it's always been such a
struggle for your pa to make out atall. Nobody
works harder than Papa, you know that."

"Mr. Shane works, too," Enie defended him.
"Just because he docs it different . . . It must be
better than Papa's way, looks to me like."

"Now, don't run down your own, Earline,"

Mamma said sternly. "Some have better luck than others," she finished, a little lamely.

Better sense, too, Enie thought, but didn't say so. The baby cried and Mamma took her up to nurse her. Mamma looked thoughtfully at Enie. "I got a notion it's the hard time your pa's had that makes him get his back up so easy. You younguns never knowed what it's like not to be able to put your hand to ary thing you can call you own. Our house might not be fine as some, but it's ours, free and clear. It took harder work from Papa to make it like that then you will ever know—and the little land he owns means a heap when he can recollect *his* young days, share-croppin'. Movin' from place to place, never one better than the last, sometimes worse. Piling your house plunder in an old wagon and movin' on. I got this notion that it does something to a man he can't get over soon. Maybe never." She sighed. "It's a habit that sets in him— hitting out at everything and anything that reminds him."

Enie stood, sullen faced, under Mamma's rebuke. She said coldly, "People can be rich and still have trouble." Mamma flashed her a sharp look, then sighed again.

———————

The crazy summer, heavy with Enie's rebellion and dreaming, wore toward its close and, suddenly, there was the excitement of getting ready for another school year.

Papa bought stout brown oxfords and two pairs of brown cotton stockings for Enie at the Emporium in Green Pine, and Mamma let her pick out the print for a new dress. When she started to sew the material, though, the belt on the old machine broke. T.H. patched it neatly with a bit of harness, then the thread Papa had bought but one spool of ran out and Enie had to go to Miss Katy's store for more.

"I hate to send you so far in this heat," Mamma said, "but my hands are purely tied till I get thread. Don't walk too fast, but don't dawdle, neither. I'm short enough of time as it is."

Enie was glad to go. It would take her away from the house for an hour, and Miss Katy's store was always a treat. After the glare of the long, hot walk she had to blink a moment in its shadowiness before she could make out the jar of jawbreakers on the show case, or the packs of chewing gum lined up neatly inside. When she was over her sun blindness she looked round with the interest that was fresh each time she came to the store.

A rack of aprons and house dresses stood against one wall; a row of shelves in the rear held stacks of overalls, flat cardboard boxes of sewing thread, shoe boxes, yard goods, and a fascinating welter of odds-and-ends Miss Katy bought from the peddler whose little truck chugged along the Tired Creek-Pleasant Grove road twice a year.

Gallon jugs of turpentine and a huge drum of kerosene stood on the floor along the wall opposite the dress rack. Over in one corner was the little wire cage at whose window you could buy money orders and postage stamps.

The back door leading to Miss Katy's living quarters stood open and a scent of simmering meat stole through the store, making Enie's mouth water; the Singletons hardly ever had beef, and this was surely beef. Miss Katy looked up from the sewing in her lap.

"Well, hey there, Enie. You haven't been to see me in I don't know when. How is everybody at your house?"

"All tollable, thank you ma'am," Enie answered politely. "Mamma's sewing, too—on my new school dress, and she ran out of thread." She held the sample out, moist from her palm, and Miss Katy's myopic eyes squinted at it as she laid her work aside and got up from the low rocking chair.

"Does that look like a match to you? Looks darker on the spool, but it'll sew up lighter."

Enie inspected the spool Miss Katy fished from the box. As she laid her nickel on the counter she caught herself looking sideways at the candy jar, and her face grew hot when Miss Katy's hand slipped into the wide mouth of the jar. Leeroy did love jawbreakers, but she hadn't meant to hint—even with a look.

"You take these to the younguns," Miss Katy

directed, reaching for a paper sack. "And here's a pack of gum for you."

"Oh, I don't care about any, Miss Katy," Enie lied, but Miss Katy dropped a pack of chewing gum in with the candy and thread. "Pshaw, I reckon you're not so grown up you can't enjoy a stick of chewing gum!" And there was nothing for Enie to do but murmur "Thank you, ma'am," and take the sack. People said it was a wonder Miss Katy made a living out of her store, giving half the stock away to younguns like she did; but no one had ever heard her complain of being hard-up. Mamma said Miss Katy was one of the souls God put in the world to even up the good and evil, and Enie thought there might well be something to Mamma's theory as she passed the red gasoline pump in the yard and started back along the hot, long road.

5

THE NEW English teacher was also Enie's home room teacher. Her name was Cecily Pritchard and she was small and very young-looking, but a quiet authority emanated from her in the first words she spoke and in her self-assured, no-nonsense manner that kept even the smart-alecky big boys in line.

At recess some of the girls glibly gave out information about the new teacher—most of which, Enie suspected, was without foundation. Her age, dress, shoes and hair style were of major interest to the adolescent girls clustered under the big oak. But it was Mary Lee William's statement that fired Enie with excitement almost too great to be contained. Mary Lee's father, Green Pine's leading druggist, was on the school board—a fact Mary Lee did not let the others forget. With a toss of her curly brown head and flash of dimples she said, knowingly, "Miss Pritchard lives in North Carolina in some little town like this, but she went to college in New York City. I heard Daddy tell Mother so. That's why she's so stylish."

Enie, who always felt on the fringe of the town girls' gatherings anyway, withdrew to think this over. She had never known anyone who had been to New York City! Even the Shanes settled for New Orleans, Mobile, Montgomery. She was still tingling with thrills when the bell rang and the home room noisily settled for the first day's work.

Right from the start Miss Pritchard took an interest in Enie as no teacher had before. It began with the first assignment she gave the class. She told them to write a composition, but gave them no subject or choice of suggested ones. It was an unheard-of procedure and promptly threw the students into a sea of consternation. Mary Lee Williams looked as blank as the rest, though she was smart and had always reigned like a little queen with teachers and students alike. Enie had always outstripped Mary Lee scholastically— sometimes by the narrowest margin—but the better grades were cold comfort when she had to endure the town girl's condescending manner year after year with never a real triumph of her own to alleviate the discomfort.

At recess that day Mary Lee left her town friends in their usual tight circle and approached Enie with an ingratiating smile. "Look, Earline, what are you going to write about for tomorrow's English?" Enie could feel Lou Addie's and Carol's eyes switch from the boys' side of the playground to her.

"I don't know. I hadn't thought about it." It was true; aside from the little quiver of interest when Miss Pritchard made the assignment, she had not given it a thought. Her composition book at home was full of scribbling that might easily furnish an idea if she had need of it. But she could not tell this to Mary Lee Williams; her composition book was as private and personal as a diary.

The dimple in Mary Lee's round cheek disappeared. "I don't see why she couldn't at least give us a title," she said, crossly. Enie moved uneasily, scuffing gravel with her ugly, heavy shoes. "Look, Earline," Mary Lee wheedled, "you could write something—just the beginning—for me. I can finish it, easy, if you will. It's just getting started that's so hard." The dimple flashed back. "I'll do something nice for you sometime, if you will."

Enie knew it had not been easy for Mary Lee Williams to ask a favor of her; at the same time she had a lightning vision of the advantages that might be hers if she chose to grant it. It was such a little thing to do and would cost her so little that she was half-surprised to hear her own voice answering, "No. No, I can't. I've got my own to write. You'll have to do yours, Mary Lee—like everybody else.

Mary Lee's face turned crimson. She opened her

mouth to say something, closed it without saying anything and stalked angrily back to her friends.

The day after the compositions were turned in, Miss Pritchard devoted most of the period to poetry: its meaning and spirit. She explained smilingly that poetry did not have to rhyme—and that a rhyme was not necessarily a poem. "Prose frequently contains the beauty, the spirit of poetry," she said, glancing at the tiny gold watch on her wrist. "We have a minute or two before the bell. I'd like to give you an example that may illustrate better than what I've said—better, I think, than an essay written by someone you will never see and can think of only as someone dead and belonging to a faraway past."

She picked the sheaf of papers from her desk, slipped one from the elastic band that held them together. "This was written by a member of our own class—Earline Singleton. She has called it 'Imagination.'"

Before the light gasps of surprise had fluttered to silence, Miss Pritchard began to read: "My little brother told me of a pool he found in our woods. It was very, very deep, he said, and covered with ice. He said that when he looked at the frozen pool a long time he could see silver fishes swimming in silver rings beneath the ice. He said he heard music beneath the ice—distant and of an unearthly sweetness. When I searched for the pool, it was not there. I think I had known it would not be, yet I do not believe my brother lied to me."

Enie sat staring at her desk, not seeing its scars and ink stains, only hearing with burning ears Miss Pritchard reading the words she had written in her old composition book in her secret place behind the willows sometime last summer. Miss Pritchard's voice stopped and there was a peculiar hush. Enie could feel the eyes of every student upon her, making her hotter and hotter. The bell shattered the silence; there was the clatter of feet, the rustle of papers, the thwack of a dropped book. As Enie passed the teacher's desk, Miss Pritchard touched her shoulder. "You didn't mind, did you, Earline?" she asked, and Enie said on a caught breath, "No, ma'am."

Mary Lee Williams was waiting in the hall with her bosom friend, Hilda Reese. Her face was white with rage; her dark eyes raked Enie with hate. "Teacher's pet," she hissed. "You think you're something now, don't you? A big shot. Well, that doesn't stop you being a little old country tack!" Her eyes swept contemptuously over Enie's faded cotton dress with the hem that had been let out, showing a different shade of blue, the cotton stockings and ugly, sensible shoes. She thrust her arm through Hilda's so violently that both girls' friendship bracelets jingled, and turned a furious back on Enie.

Enie's adolescent pride staggered beneath the blow. All the way home on the bus she tried to salve it with Miss Pritchard's public praise. Mary Lee's wounding words were nothing, she told herself, against Miss Pritchard's. Always, before, her good marks had been their own reward; never had a teacher in the town school praised her before the class, making her achievement a shining example. Hadn't she said in front of them all that it was a better illustration than the writing of a dead and famous author? But the wound ached in spite of the praise; it left a deep and ugly scar, and what had been friction before settled into a cold and heavy enmity. It was not till late November that things came to a head between Enie and Mary Lee Williams.

Fifty cents mysteriously disappeared from Mary Lee's desk; Miss Pritchard allowed time for everyone in the room to take part in the search for it, but the money could not be found. Enie, secretly rather pleased at Mary Lee's misfortune, busied herself studiously while the search was going on.

"Perhaps you dropped it on your way to school," Miss Pritchard suggested, but Mary Lee was positive she had laid the two quarters on her desk. "Right by the inkwell," she said, and sent a flashing glance round the room. "Right where anybody could see it if they . . ."

"That will do, Mary Lee," Miss Pritchard stopped her. "I'm sure that if anyone finds the money, it will be returned to you."

At recess a group of girls were standing round

the washbowl in the girls' basement, taking turns at the mirror, when Enie hurried in with just time to wash her hands before the bell. In her haste she did not notice the silence that fell upon the town girls as she pushed past them to the washbowl. As she laid two coins on the ledge of the bowl and turned the spigot, a gasp went up, and something clicked in Enie's brain. It was then she knew it was going to happen. She could feel a gathering together of herself in readiness, yet she did not turn and look at the girls behind her—Hilda, Juanita, Paula and Mary Lee. A cold, unflustered fury took possession of her, making her actions precise and careful and unhurried: the drawing out of a paper towel, the wiping of her hands. Mary Lee's voice, asking the question, had the silkiness of a cat's purr.

"Would you mind telling me where you got that money?"

Enie gave a last rub with the damp piece of paper, then turned her eyes upon Mary Lee. "I got it from Louise Johnson and Carrie Knowles. They owed it for sugar cane I let them have over a month ago. Just about ten minutes ago they paid me—twenty-five cents apiece for five stalks of cane apiece." It occurred to Enie that she had not heard this particular voice of hers since the last time she and Henry Jim had a roll-and-tumble fight for which they had both been soundly whipped by Mamma. "If you don't believe me you can ask them. Right now. Go ahead, why don't you?" She took a step toward Mary Lee. Through the humming in her ears, she heard Mary Lee's voice, sounding thin and queer.

"I don't need to, thank you. I know some folks in this school are always mighty hard up for change."

Enie's hand cracked resoundingly across Mary Lee's cheek. Mary Lee's shriek echoed back from the concrete walls of the basement, and Enie slapped again—again—again. She struck Mary Lee for accusing her of stealing, for the hurts and humiliations of this year and those before it. She knew she had an overwhelming advantage over the sheltered, pampered only child who had never had to defend herself against tough-fisted brothers and who boasted no heritage of red hair and the temper that went with it.

The bell jangled across the bedlam about the washbowl. The other girls' squeals mingled with Mary Lee's cries that sank to moans and hysterical sobs as Enie wound up the battle with a vicious yank of the permanently waved hair falling about Mary Lee's shoulders, picked up her two quarters and walked out, leaving the babel of horror and indignation behind her.

Her ears still hummed and there was a sick spot spreading through the middle of her. But she wasn't sorry for what she'd done; she was glad. Something really terrible would happen now; maybe she would be expelled from the school— Mary Lee's father was a member of the board—

and the disgrace would include Mamma and break her heart with disappointment and shame. But Enie was even with Mary Lee Williams; she had paid her back for all the meanness—right down to the briefest glance which had emphasized Enie's shabby clothes, each ringing blow ramming the hated words "country tack" down Mary Lee's howling throat.

The last stragglers scuffed through the door of Miss Pritchard's room, and Enie crept along behind them and slid into her seat. The shuffling and whispering gradually died into comparative silence. Miss Pritchard was writing on the blackboard and had not seen the four empty seats.

The door flew open and agitated steps crossed the room to the blackboard. Every ear strained to catch the whispered words Juanita was pouring at Miss Pritchard. Enie saw bewilderment swallow the teacher's face. She laid the chalk on the ledge of the board. "Study quietly, please," she told the class. "Come with me, Earline."

Not a word was spoken as the two girls and Miss Pritchard walked the length of the hall and descended the stairs into the carbolic aroma of the basement. Enie couldn't think and she had no feeling other than the faint sickness in her stomach. She had never been in trouble at school. She knew, in a detached sort of way, that each leaden step was bringing her closer to her doom, but she felt neither regret nor fear.

Paula, Hilda, and Mary Lee were sitting on the

wooden bench that ran alongside the wall next to the basins. Mary Lee sobbed softly, her brown curls falling untidily over the hands that covered her face.

"You'd better go upstairs, girls," Miss Pritchard said. "All but Mary Lee and Earline. You're late, as it is." The three girls trailed disappointedly out. Their steps on the stairs, their subdued twitterings drifted back, grew fainter and died. "Sit down, Earline," Miss Pritchard directed, not looking at Enie. "Stop crying, Mary Lee." Miss Pritchard took a handkerchief from the pocket of her blouse, pressed it into Mary Lee's hand. "I want you to tell me exactly what happened."

Mary Lee gave a hiccup and raised her face. She shook her hair back and fingered the scarlet weal on her cheek. "Go on, tell me," Miss Pritchard prompted. Enie stared at the gray wall opposite. Her legs had begun to tremble and she braced her feet to hide the telltale quivering of her skirt.

"*This* is what happened," Mary Lee cried, her voice shaking with outrage. "She slapped me in the face! *Earline Singleton*. She hit me and hit me till I know my jaw's broke," and she wailed in renewed anguish.

Miss Pritchard put a hand on either side of Mary Lee's face. She pressed gently, her attention all on Mary Lee; Enie might have been out at Tired Creek for all the notice Miss Pritchard took of her. "Your jaw isn't broken, but there is an ugly mark on your cheek. It's a pity—such a pretty face, too." Mollified, Mary Lee blinked through her tears. She dabbed at her eyes with Miss Pritchard's handkerchief, gave a gratified sniff at the violet scent of it. "Why did Earline slap your face, Mary Lee? What could have caused her to do such a thing?"

Mary Lee began to twist the handkerchief. Her lips parted, closed. "Ask her," she muttered at last.

"No," Miss Pritchard said. "I asked you."

"She—I—my two quarters . . ." Mary Lee began, her face reddening evenly, so the print of the blows was lost. "Well, I had this fifty cents and it disappeared off of my desk and . . ." She bogged down, pulling nervously at the handkerchief.

"You believed Earline had taken your money? You accused her of—*stealing* it?"

Mary Lee's lip trembled. "I—I never said—I just . . ."

Miss Pritchard frowned, musingly. "It's odd—I was under the impression you were such a well-bred girl. I've thought of you as—a lady. Your home, and your parents, your advantages . . . How could the loss of fifty cents make you forget yourself and all that's expected of you?"

Mary Lee looked sullenly at the wall. Miss Pritchard sighed, and Enie saw genuine sadness settle over her face. A feeling of guilt crept over Enie, guilt and tightness like grief in her throat. She jumped when Miss Pritchard's voice penetrated her welling misery. "Wasn't it really more than losing the money?"

She turned her look upon Enie, and under it Enie felt tears sting her lids. "And more for you, Earline, than the accusation? That's reason for anger, I grant you. But to strike out and do bodily hurt to anyone—I would never have believed you could behave so badly, either of you."

Silence drew out, heavy and painful, and Enie's trembling increased; the tears that had burned her lids crept out and down her pale cheeks. Miss Pritchard laid one hand on Enie's knee, the other on Mary Lee's. "I think the real problem is one you have in common. Jealousy isn't a pretty word and it isn't a pretty characteristic. It's unworthy of you both. I'd like to be proud of the two brightest students this year has given me."

She stood up and smoothed her skirt. "Now, wash your faces and report to class." And she walked out of the basement and up the stairs.

Enie was the first to speak, her prime feeling one of surprise that the whole episode had suddenly become childish and unimportant. "I'm sorry I slapped you, Mary Lee."

"Well, I'm—I'm sorry I—made you mad," Mary Lee returned after a brief hesitation. She gave a last sad little sniff. Awkwardly they stood up, moved toward the washbowl. Mary Lee touched her cheek tenderly, and began to comb her hair.

"I love Miss Pritchard!" Enie burst out.

Mary Lee carefully applied lipstick. "Golly," she

murmured when she had finished, "she didn't even *offer* to punish us."

"I reckon she thought we punished ourselves enough," Enie replied thoughtfully.

Mary Lee screwed the cap onto her lipstick. She drew a deep breath and said in a rush, not looking at Enie, "I'm sorry I've been mean to you before this."

Above, a bell rang, the echo of feet scraped along the halls, sounding far away. The two girls went sedately up the stairs, side by side.

6

JUST BEFORE CHRISTMAS, it turned bitterly cold. A harsh, dry wind roared through the tops of the oaks, found knotholes and cracks in the house and blew its cold breath through them. The branch froze over, and Leeroy coughed at night so Enie could not sleep. All up and down the creek, farmers were butchering pigs, and the screams of the doomed beasts sounded, high and terrible sometimes, above the wind. Every Tired Creek kitchen smelled, tantalizingly, of boiling spareribs and backbone, of frying chitlings, and in the smokehouses hams and sausages hung over the slow hickory fires.

Tired Creek was not a community to bedeck itself for Christmas. The creek ran cold and sluggish, flanked by cold, bare land with its few brown cornstalks and stumps of cut cane. A few giant sunflowers, dead and brittle, remained standing in a few bleak yards. The houses stood, blank-eyed, shut tight against the cold. But the night before Christmas a little pine tree beside the Shanes' front steps blossomed with the lovely garish fruit of Christmas: colored lights, a luminous star, an angel with shimmering wings.

Henry Jim, coming from the store, told of it at home, and after supper the Singletons walked down the road to see it. Enie tucked the baby in a nest of blankets in Leeroy's wagon, and Papa carried Sue Ann on his shoulder. Leeroy scampered ahead, wild with excitement, and T.H. followed sheepishly behind the others, half ashamed of such foolishness. They stood on the edge of the road opposite the gate in the myrtle hedge and looked at the glittering pine tree.

"Now, that's a pretty thing, I declare," Mamma murmured, and looking up in the winter dusk, Enie saw her face ashine with childlike pleasure.

"Hit is a right pretty sight," Papa admitted, but when Sue Ann echoed, "Pitty sight," he added, disapprovingly, "Must cost a mint o' money to burn them lights on top of all the others blazin' away in the house."

"He's got it to burn," T.H. said. And though she dared not say so, Enie thought it was a beautiful way to use money—burn it like that. She could hear strains of music drifting from the house and knew the Shanes must be having one of their company parties, with Rowan home from school and the relatives from Mobile spending Christmas with them.

They looked at the tree and the house and listened to the muted sounds of gaiety till the cold began to pinch, and even so they had to drag Leeroy, stamping and whining till Papa threatened to warm his britches for him if he didn't shut up. Night settled down, raw and sharp, a few stars blinked—pallid after the lights on the tree and in Shanes' windows—and the walk home seemed longer with the tree getting farther behind them. At home, though, the kitchen was warm from the embers in the stove. Papa went ahead to light the lamp, and the others groped after him. The smell of Mamma's baking lingered and the pot of backbone still slowly simmered. Mamma gave each of them a piece of gingerbread and a glass of buttermilk.

It was still pitch dark when Enie woke from Leeroy's poking her ribs. She flopped over to see him, a dim shape, sitting up in bed. His face was turned toward the pale square of the window and he was trembling, so that the bed shook. Enie sat up beside him. "What is it, Leeroy? What's the matter?"

"I scen him. Jest now. I *seen* him," Leeroy's teeth chattered.

"Saw who, Leeroy? Saw, not seen."

"Old Sandy Claus is who! He—he went right through that window. I ain't telling no lie, Enie. Cross my heart and hope to die, I sure seen him."

"You couldn't've, Leeroy. You know . . ."

"I did," Leeroy wailed.

"Hush up," Enie hissed. "You want to wake up everybody?"

"But I did see him. He was goin' through that window there!"

"Well . . ."

"He brung my bicycle! I heard it a-bumping against the door—so big he couldn't hardly get it in the house. I didn't know what it was at first, then I seen him goin' through the window and I know that bike is in the kitchen. That is sure where he left it at. Let's slip in there and see it, Enie, right now."

Enie didn't know what to do. There was no bicycle, of course. She thought she had convinced Leeroy that there would be no bicycle this year; he had appeared to accept the fact, and now here he was, all of a tremble with implicit faith. She put her arm around him and tried to draw him against her.

"Look, Leeroy, listen to me, sugar. You know there isn't really any Santa Claus. Henry Jim told you last Christmas—when you weren't hardly five years old! Don't you recollect?"

"I don't care. I seen him. Jest a minnit ago."

Enie gave him a hard squeeze. "You must've dreamt it. Somebody made all that up about Santa Claus, a long, long time ago. It's like the fairy stories and all. Christmas presents are from your mamma and papa. A bicycle costs—I don't know

70

what it costs—twenty-five dollars, I bet. Papa wouldn't have that much cash money, ever." She felt Leeroy stiffen, try to pull away. "Lie down and let me cover you up. It's not daylight yet."

But Leeroy would not lie down. He stopped trembling and did not talk any more, but his thin little body in the flannel nightgown remained rigidly upright.

"If you'll lie down, Leeroy, I'll tell you a story. I'll tell you *The King of the Golden River.*" It had been Leeroy's favorite story ever since Enie first read it to him out of her sixth grade reader. He slid reluctantly under the quilts. "Scrooch up close to me," Enie told him. Leeroy moved close and Enie began the story, her throat aching from having to whisper and from its hurt for Leeroy. Before she got to the end she stopped to see if he had fallen asleep, and her ear caught the little animal sound of Leeroy sucking his thumb. He had stopped more than a year ago when he mashed his thumb in the smokehouse door; this was the first time Enie had ever known him to go back to the old consolation.

It was still dark when Enie heard Papa start clattering the stove lids. The baby cried and she heard Mamma taking her into bed with her to nurse her. Leeroy slept. Enie, looking at the shadow of his lashes on his blue-white cheek, wished he could sleep and dream the whole of the day away. She wished she could do the same. The mean winter dawn seeped blearily into the room and

Enie's teeth chattered while she dressed. Leeroy crawled out from under the quilts and took his clothes into the kitchen to put them on behind the stove.

The family gathered for breakfast. No one said, "Merry Christmas"; it was just like all the other Christmases except for the tightness in Enie's throat. After they had eaten, Papa brought the parcels, wrapped in brown store paper, from the front room and handed them round, solemnly. A little awkward, a little embarrassed, the young Singletons opened them. Enie forced herself to look at Leeroy, after she had thanked Papa for her good, serviceable wool sweater.

He sat at the far end of the bench, his arms spread on the table. Between them he had arranged three tiny tin vehicles: a bright blue sedan, a yellow roadster, and a scarlet tractor with a tiny man that could be taken out of the driver's seat and put back again. Leeroy's eyes did not move from the toys, though Enie watched him a long time. Not that day nor at any time thereafter did he ever refer to his dream of Santa Claus and the bicycle.

———————

All winter there had been trouble between Papa and T.H. Enie thought it had been working up ever since T.H. turned sixteen and got so tall. He took Papa's carping criticism, his shouted threats, in sullen silence, but something smoldered beneath the silence—something that made Enie tremble sometimes, and Mamma look nervously from father to son. T.H. was Papa's equal in height and his shoulders had filled out some this year, relieving him of the bean-pole look of the tall adolescent. His good Sunday suit had to be altered and passed down to Henry Jim, and Papa had been loud in his complaint of the cost of a new suit for T.H. Mamma had hopes of T.H. staying in school till he finished; he had only one year to go after this one. He had never liked school or done well in his studies, but Enie had to admit he was smart enough in some ways. He could make a little model airplane to perfection, usually assembling his own patterns because the ready-made ones were too expensive for him to buy. And he could draw anything that had to do with a motor, and repair just about any kind of machinery. He was always wanting Papa to buy a tractor; he said nobody could farm nowadays without one.

Late on a January afternoon Papa caught T.H. rolling a cigarette when he was supposed to be at chores in the barn. The roar of Papa's infuriated voice came through the closed kitchen window, and both Mamma and Enie went to the window and saw Papa follow T.H. into the woodshed. With all her nerves gathered into a tight knot, Enie waited for the sound of the strap on T.H.'s back, but she heard only Papa's voice, still raised in anger, lecturing T.H.

"I reckon you think you're pretty smart, smokin', maybe samplin' a jug off in the woods, too. You've not been foolin' me with your slinkin' in late of nights. How do I know you've not been up Big Washout way, foolin' round Atkinses' girls?" If he gave T.H. a chance to answer, Enie could not hear it. "You're agettin' too big for yore britches lately, and I aim to show you right now about how big you are." The sound Enie waited for came then, and between the blows Papa's words, interspersed with panting grunts . . . "Show you" . . . thwack . . . "no boy of mine" . . . thwack . . . "takin' tobacco don't b'long to you" . . . thwack . . . "goin' to the devil" . . . thwack . . .

Enie pressed her forehead against the cold pane, saw the dry leaves moved by the wind in the oak tree, a puff of cold dust near the lot fence. T.H.'s voice, cut with a sob but a man's voice nevertheless, came out of the shed. "That's enough. You hit me for the last time!"

Mamma turned from the window, but Enie could not move; it was as if her feet were fastened to the floor. She heard Papa roar, "Talk back, will you? Talk back to your father. I'll give you something you'll . . ."

"You won't give me another licking with that strop. I've taken my last one—off you or anybody else," T.H. cried hoarsely.

Behind her, Enie heard Mamma trying to distract the children's attention, but Enie clung to the scene before her. Something was happening out

74

there in the dread place of punishment—something terrible but of tremendous significance. Papa had gone too far this time, and a sort of elation mingled with the terror in Enie; she had to see it through. The rumble of Papa's voice went on and on in the shed, though she could no longer distinguish the words. After a while she saw him come out. Before he stepped onto the porch, he straightened his shoulders, and when he came into the kitchen he was putting his feet down hard and mad, as always after he had administered a whipping. Stealing a look at his face, however, Enie saw trouble in it—something deeper than anger, an uncertainty, as if he didn't know what to do next, as if *he* had taken the licking.

Henry Jim came in the front of the house, down the hall, and stopped in the doorway. Papa turned on him in a measure of relief. "Let me see any more of that kinda goings on and more fur's going to fly," he bellowed. "You get big notions next, let me tell you right now, boy, you better not try no monkeyshines round me like yore smart-alecky brother!"

He doesn't know, Enie thought. Papa doesn't know we heard T.H. turn on him. He's not the boss of T.H. any more and he knows it. But Henry Jim will turn, too—if he has to. Maybe next year, maybe the next. And so will I . . . And she felt a wild excitement pouring through her.

T.H. didn't come to supper that night. Papa ate with his eyes on his plate, stopping only to touch

Sue Ann's head when she laid it against his knee. Sometime late in the night Enie woke to hear T.H. creep to the room where he and Henry Jim slept.

After school the next day Papa told T.H. to mend the broken place in the lot fence. Enie looked up from her homework to see if T.H. was going to give Papa an argument; he said nothing, just went to the shed for tools and began working on the fence. Pape went about his business and Enie forgot everything but the work she was concentrating upon. It was dark when Mamma told her to put her books away and set the table. Papa stamped across the porch and flung the door open, glaring around the kitchen. "Where's T.H.?" he demanded.

Mamma turned from the stove. "He was workin' on the fence, like you told him to."

"He left his chore half done like he always does," Papa said through his teeth. "Left the tools layin' in the yard to rust an' ruin."

"He might've stepped out back," Mamma pleaded in the delicate way in which she referred to the privy. "You got no call to be so hard on him, Clement."

"Got no call, have I? I think diff'rent. He's out to show his biggitiness, but he'll not get away with it. I'm boss here, long as he puts his feet under my table." He turned to Henry Jim. "Go see can you find him. Tell him I got business with him." As he threw himself into his chair, Papa added, "I'll take the devil outa that boy if it's the last thing I do."

But Papa did not take the devil out of T.H. Not that night nor any other. Henry Jim came in, bug-eyed, to say he wasn't on the place; he'd looked everywhere—even down the road a piece—and there wasn't a sign of him.

Mamma flung her apron over her face, and Papa looked as if someone had thrown a bucket of cold water over his, his anger giving way to a stupid stare that finally found his plate, which Enie hastened to fill with grits and ham gravy. Later, lying beside Leeroy and his little tractor, Enie heard Mamma talking to Papa in a broken voice. "He's run off from home, Clem. I know it, I feared it after last night."

"He'll run back fast enough, too, when his belly gets empty," Papa retorted, but his blustering was empty as a bubble.

"That don't stop him from getting into trouble first. You've not been patient enough, Clem. Boys have to try theirselves a little bit when they're growin' up." Mamma sounded close to tears.

"The Book says spare the rod and spoil the child, don't it? I never spared the rod and I never spoilt a child. I do my duty the way I see it. Long as he eat my grub and lived under my roof . . ."

"It's grub and shelter he earned in hard work," Mamma broke in. "You don't have enough patience with these younguns, an' that's the purentee truth. You got to gentle a boy that age like you would a fractious mule."

"I've whipped sense into more'n one mule, haven't I?"

"Just the same," Mamma said after a little silence, "it didn't work, this time."

That held Papa for a moment, and Mamma went on talking—so low that Enie couldn't catch most of the words, only the half-sob that occasionally punctuated their flow. At last Papa groaned, rolling over so violently that he made the bedstead bump the wall. "Cain't you let a tard man get his sleep? Nag, nag, nag."

"I'm worried," Mamma said then, her voice loud and naked with fear. "You'd ought to be, too. T.H. was our first little youngun, Clement, and the dear Lord only knows where he is at, this night. Out in the cold and dark, in some trouble for all we know," and she began to weep, making the goose-pimples rise on Enie, lying helplessly in the dark.

When morning came, T.H. had not come home. Mamma, heavy-eyed and distraught, served breakfast, which they all ate in silence, even Sue Ann's prattle instinctively hushed. Papa did not look at anyone, and Enie and Henry Jim bolted their food and hurried out to wait for the school bus.

That night in the middle of supper—another silent, dragging meal—Mamma suddenly spoke out. "You got to do something, Clem. He might be staying in town. Mr. Kelly has give him jobs at the garage ever now and then . . ."

"Let him stay in town if he likes it better than

his own home," Papa retorted, but he chewed his lips and the anger in his eyes had turned to a sullen worry.

"Mr. Tom Shane . . ." Mamma proffered tremulously, "he might be able to help us locate him. He'd know how to go about it."

"I don't need Tom Shane's help," Papa snapped. "I'll not go begging to anybody. You want a scandal on our name? We never had ary thing said against us, yet—which is more'n Shane can say."

Mamma rose from her untouched meal; her tear-reddened eyes flashed at Papa. "You're a hard man, Clement Singleton, if I do say so before your children." Enie held her breath, expecting Papa to fly out at Mamma, but he only took a mouthful of stewed okra and sopped the slimy juice from his plate with a bit of corn pone.

The next day Mr. Orin Thompson, the mail carrier, left a letter in the Singleton's box. It was addressed to Mamma in T.H.'s handwriting and had been mailed from Green Pine. Enie found it in the box at the edge of the road when she alighted from the school bus.

"Read it to me, Enie," Mamma whispered, coming round the ironing board to sink into a chair. "He's all right, thank the Lord, if he's wrote a letter."

"Dear Ma," T.H. had written in pencil on rough tablet paper, *"I have got a little time*

before the bus comes to take me away from this crummy hole. I want you to know I am not mad at anybody any more, not even Pa. He's the way he is and I am the way I am and we cannot get along, so it is best like this. I been wanting to strike out on my own a long time but was too young and there was nothing in the way of jobs from all we could hear, as you know. Now it looks better and I am old enough. Not a kid and have not been for a year at least. So I am going to get a job with a man Mr. Kelly give me his name, I will not say where. He (Mr. K.) would of give me a place with him but did not have one open. It is better like this I am sure, not being so near if Pa took a notion to make trouble. There is nothing he can do anyhow, you can tell him. I will be working for wages and making my way in the world. Don't worry about me Ma as this is what I want and aim to have. Maybe it is a good thing it all happened. You want me to finish school I know but I will learn more this way and doing what I want besides. Don't worry about me getting sick or anything as I have never been sick a day in my life yet and tell Pa not to feel hard to-wards Mr. K. as he tried to talk me into going home but no soap so he done what he could to help me get work. I have thought this over and did not jump into it in a temper else I would of left that same night. I come by the bus fare honest so do not worry. May be I can send something home out of my pay now and then to help out if I am lucky. Your son T.H."

Mamma's tears ran down her cheeks like rain as Enie refolded the letter and laid it on the ironing board. "Don't take on so, Mamma," she begged. "He's all right. Like he says, it's maybe better it happened."

Papa ranted violently and long after he read T.H.'s letter. He threatened to put the law on Mr. Kelly for aiding and abetting a minor to run away from home; he heaped recriminations upon Mamma for siding with a youngun against his blood father whose bounden duty it was to use the rod and not spoil the child; and he called T.H. an ungrateful, feisty young one who had taken his father's care and keep for more than sixteen years, only to throw it back in his teeth and hightail it when he was big enough to be of some help. He wound the tirade up by forbidding T.H.'s name to be spoken again in his presence, and a haggard peace descended upon the household.

For months Mamma looked constantly to hear from T.H. again, but no word came. Enie's heart swelled with envy. T.H. was seeing the world; she felt it in her bones. Lucky T.H., to be a boy and ruthless enough to cut all cords that sought to bind him.

7

———————

BEFORE SCHOOL WAS OUT Miss Pritchard and Enie had a talk which glowed like a jewel in Enie's mind all summer long. It was not the first one; all through the year Miss Pritchard had been arranging these little conferences over Enie's work, binding teacher and pupil in a relationship Enie would never forget.

It was recess time—for bus pupils could not be kept after school—and the classroom was empty save for those two, the dark head and the red one bent over the little pile of compositions on Miss Pritchard's desk.

"I think your writing shows real promise, Earline," Miss Pritchard said. "I hope you'll keep in practice during vacation. Write your thoughts, your observations, keep at it, form the habit. Never scorn the things you *know*, the things around you every day. Nothing's insignificant if you do it well enough." She looked at Enie in silence a moment, then asked, "Have you ever thought you might be a writer, someday?"

Enie caught her breath.

"I—No, ma'am. I reckon I never really thought that. I just always liked making things up in my head, using words I wasn't used to hearing. Writing them down made me remember." She flushed. "I might not be able to get a very good education."

"That needn't keep you from writing," Miss Pritchard said quickly, "some very fine writers have had very little formal education. Learning has all sorts of sources. Get all the schooling you can, surely. But don't forget that life itself is the great teacher. Maybe that sounds like a bit of sermonizing, but you'll see. Don't neglect looking—really seeing things, everything!—and listening. You'd be surprised how few people really know how to listen, but I think you do. Keep your mind as open and alert as it is now, Earline, and keep writing—if that's what you really want with all your heart."

"Oh, it is," Enie cried, knowing suddenly that it was true. It was what she wanted most. Getting away from Tired Creek, becoming a teacher, seeing snow and mountains and the ocean, achieving the mastery of words that swept her into another world with their magic, were all means to the end Miss Pritchard had with a few simple words permitted her to glimpse. How had she not known all along? Now it seemed so clear, a thing that had lain deep within her all the while she had groped and stumbled in the dark.

Enie wanted to pour out her gratitude then and there, but the words would not come. It was often so with her; words that flowed freely from her pencil would stick in her throat, tie her tongue and smite her dumb. She could only gaze, flushed and shining, into Miss Pritchard's face. But the teacher in her wisdom must have known and understood, for she smiled and, astonishingly, she bent and kissed Enie's forehead.

Mamma was on the porch, stringing little new beans, when Enie got home. Enie stepped round Jenny and Sue Ann, pouring sand in and out of tobacco tins in the middle of the walk, and flung herself onto the edge of the porch. With no lack of words, now, she told Mamma all Miss Pritchard had said.

"She thinks I might be a writer, Mamma, a real author. I might write books that'll be printed for people to read—people all over, everywhere. It don't seem possible, does it, *me* doing anything like that?"

Mamma's hands lay, stricken, in the pan of beans. She looked at Enie as if she were beholding a miracle. "I can't hardly take it in, seems like," she said, finally. "I sure am proud of you, honey. I always have been, to tell the truth. I wanted a little girl child so bad when I was carryin' you, but I'd about made up my mind I wouldn't have nothing but big old strappin' boys for Papa and the farm to rob me of! That was fine, too, but I hankered so after a baby girl to play with a little bit an' love. That's just what I done, too, when you come. And now your teacher says this about you! Well, how do I know what to think? I just hope . . ."

"Hope what, Mamma?"

"Hope things'll go good so you can get all the learnin' you'll need." She began on the beans again. "We'll have to leave it in God's hands."

But Enie, hunched on the edge of the sagging porch, had no intention of leaving it in God's hands. It was her private belief that leaving things in the hands of God was altogether too risky. And just as she was beginning to feel rebellious and mean, Mamma said firmly, "All the same, God helps them that helps theirselves. You got to keep at it and do your best, too."

If Miss Pritchard's revelation humbled Enie's rebellious spirit, it also gave her a certain self-significance. Following Miss Pritchard's counsel to look and listen, she discovered that she was looking at herself—the self beneath a surface homeliness she had come to take for granted—almost as if she were another person. If there wore things she could not have, there were also things she could at least try for; and it was on the heels of such reflection that she asked Mamma if Leeroy mightn't move in with Henry Jim and let her have a room to herself.

Mamma was silent a long moment, then said slowly, "You're too big a girl to be sleeping with your brother. I thought about it back in the winter, but . . ." She left the sentence unfinished and Enie knew she had been going to say she had hoped T.H. might come back. Mamma's granting her request now told Enie that she no longer hoped. T.H. had taken himself out of their midst and if he ever returned, it would be only to visit. Sometimes Mamma acted as if T.H. had died, but Enie was impatient of such an attitude. T.H. had done what he had to do; it was the only thing Enie had ever found to admire him for.

She moved Leeroy's clothes into the bureau drawer that had held T.H.'s things. She felt excited and happy—and a little sad, too. With loving hands she stacked the few faded shirts, the patched undergarments he seldom wore in the summer, the three pairs of overalls with patched knees. Enie closed the drawer, half lonely for Leeroy already. But that night, lying in the double bed alone, she felt giddy with luxury. She stretched, rolled over and flung her legs out, testing her freedon with a fine abandon.

Next, Enie tackled Mamma about cutting her hair. "I can't go on wearing these pigtails forever. They look so dumb and—childish." She wound the braids in a coronet and inspected her reflection with some satisfaction, but Mamma said it made her face all eyes.

"Then let me cut it, Mamma," Enie teased.

"Nobody wears pigtails these days, nobody my age anyhow. Fourteen's not so young." She wondered what Mamma would say if she knew Otis Jason had asked Enie to take a walk with him after dinner-on-the-ground at the all-day singing last month. She hadn't done it because of the rash of pimples on Otis's forehead and the big drops of sweat on his upper lip. She hadn't wanted to hurt his feelings and had told him, politely, that she had to look after Sue Ann.

Enie pestered Mamma about her hair till Mamma told her in exasperation to go ahead and chop it off to the bone if she was bound to, she'd have nobody to blame but herself if Papa raised the roof. Before Mamma could change her mind Enie set out for Jasons' and asked Lou Addie, who had a flair for style, to cut her hair. She did feel a little hollow inside when she saw the shining cut-off mass on the Jasons' floor. But she felt better when Lou Addie finished her shampoo and rolled up the long bobbed ends on her own kid curlers, and they sat in the porch swing and had a good talk while it dried, though Enie knew she was needed at home.

She could hardly believe her eyes when Lou Addie was done with her. No tacky little-girl pigtails skinned uncompromisingly back from her thin, big-eyed face and round forehead. The bright hair, shimmering from Lou Addie's vigorous soft-soap lathering and well-water rinsing, fell in a soft, in-curving roll upon Enie's shoulders. It seemed to

Enie that her face looked less sharp at the chin, less bulging at the brow; even the freckles seemed toned down, somehow. She couldn't thank Lou Addie enough, but Lou Addie smiled, putting her hand up to hide the discolored tooth she meant to have "fixed" when she earned the money it would cost.

"I haven't forgot all that arithmetic you worked for me, Enie. Anyhow, I love to fool with hair. I thought that page-boy style would look good on you. I might take a course in beauty culture when I finish school."

Mamma couldn't hide her pleasure and gave up the attempt when she saw how happy it made Enie to look and feel stylish. "I don't know what your papa will say," she reminded Enie uneasily.

Papa didn't even see Enie's hair till supper was over and his chair pushed back. He glared for a surprised second, then observed disgustedly, "Reckon the Book saying a woman's hair is her crowning glory don't mean nothing nowadays. All of 'em running round like shorn sheep. A man likes a female to *look* like a female."

"I haven't noticed no males with their hair cut like that," Henry Jim said daringly, blotting a last trace of gravy on his plate with a fragment of biscuit.

"And I haven't noticed anybody asked your opinion," Papa snapped, taking a toothpick and turning his back on Enie. She thought it was just as well that Papa had more important things to think and worry about than anybody's hair style.

As though the winter rains had exhausted the supply forever, spring had come on dry, and by the end of June Tired Creek was held in the fiery clutches of a drought that threatened doom to the crops. Mr. Shane had set up a temporary irrigation system and Papa said with bitterness, "He'll not lose a penny—him that could afford a loss the balance of us can't."

Enie had to admit that Papa's resentment was only human, as she lugged buckets of water in the hope of saving part of their crop. The water in the well was seriously low. Mamma scolded the little ones if they threw out a drop when they drank from the dipper. Enie carried dishwater and washwater leavings to the edge of the field and, like Papa and the other farmers, she took to scanning the sky with anxious regularity before she went to bed in the sultry dark.

Drought was always a serious thing, but this one frightened Enie for reasons of her own. If Papa lost even one crop, how could she possibly hope the money might be raised to send her to college? Even if she could somehow win him over to see the importance of such an investment. It was still three years away, but Enie knew every day of it would be needed to put by the several hundred dollars a single year of college required. It made her so desperate to think about it that she always ended by fixing her mind on other things, telling herself not to go jumping ahead but to keep her senses. A lot could happen in a year; look at her! At least two inches taller than she'd been at thirteen. She hardly ever felt like a child, this summer, and the mixed-up, crazy times of a year ago seemed now to belong to another life.

Shorthanded without T.H., Papa drove Henry Jim till his round boy's face took on the gaunt contours of a tired man's, but there was no hint of rebellion in it. Henry Jim shared Papa's respect for the land and bowed to its demands without question or complaint. Then, at last, when the nightmare of the drought had begun to seem endless, Enie woke to lightning that filled her room with violet brilliance and thunder that shook the house. Rain came roaring onto the tin roof, its sound sweeter than music. Some of the crop would be salvaged, the well wouldn't dry up.

The breaking of the drought, though it made things easier, did not eliminate the extra work caused by T.H.'s absence. When the pinch was tight, Mamma went to the field, leaving housework and babies to Enie. It did not suit Enie, who wondered if she could not use her mind to better advantage while wielding a hoe or bending her back over potato-bug picking than amid the frequent interruptions by the children.

"Let me go help Henry Jim," she begged. "I'm

young and hardy. It won't ache my back like it does yours." But Mamma was adamant.

"Field work's not good for young girls that need to have a care for their looks," she said, half teasing, yet with an undercurrent of firmness Enie knew she could not prevail against. "I've kept you to nicer chores this long, I don't aim to give in now."

Enie was by no means sure that diaper changing and washing constituted "nicer chores," but in Mamma's eyes it was so and there was nothing Enie could do about it. Jenny, who had been such a docile baby, was teething and fretful this summer, and Enie often got a meal together with the baby clutched on her hip. She pressed Leeroy into service as much as she could, but he had a way of disappearing when she needed him most and she could not take the time to hunt him up.

It was in the midst of this trying time that he unearthed the harmonica. Digging one of his trenches behind the barn, he turned it up in a trowelful of earth. It was rusty and the wood casing was cracked, but when Leeroy knocked the dirt from the vents and blew into them, something like music emerged. He was greatly excited over his discovery, took great pains to clean and polish the harmonica. He blew it in his spare time, crouched in the chinaberry tree or hidden up in the barn loft when Papa and Henry Jim were out of earshot. As the summer days passed, he got so he could oblige with just about any tune Mamma or Enie suggested. But mostly he made up his own. The sweet strains, always tinged with the mournfulness peculiar to harmonicas, made Enie faintly nostalgic. For what, she was not certain—possibly the childhood which was flowing too quickly away from Leeroy. She had felt him growing away from her for some time—or was it the other way round and was she only leaving him behind?—and it made her vaguely sad.

It was as if the harp, as Leeroy called it, was the elusive treasure for which he had dug so long, for he filled his trenches carefully and packed the soil over them so Papa wouldn't holler at him again for tearing the place up, and abandoned the pastime that had fascinated him for so long.

"That old harp must of been left here by folks that had this place fore we did," Mamma mused. "Did you notice, Enie, looked like foreign words of some kind on it?"

Enie thought it was German, but could not be sure as she knew little of foreign languages. She tried to talk with Leeroy about the harmonica, but he fell silent, as he often did with her nowadays, tapping the harmonica against the palm of his dusty little hand, his look far-off and dreaming. Despite his unwillingness to share his new interest, Enie sensed it as a bond between them; she thought his love of playing the harp was something like her love of writing stories.

About that time Enie received a post card from Miss Pritchard with a picture of the New York

Public Library on it. In the space for correspondence Miss Pritchard had written, "I have spent the day in here at work. I found myself wishing for you. Someday you will be acquainted with this building. I feel it in my bones."

Enie read the message till she knew it by heart, looked at the picture till the lions guarding the long shallow flight of steps were like old friends. "Someday . . . I feel it in my bones." It was like a promise from one who would never break her word. She hadn't even known Miss Pritchard was in New York, but the card brought them together as in the school year the talks at recess had done. She felt—miraculously—that Miss Pritchard might be right, that someday she, Earline Singleton, would be there . . .

Enie put the card under her Sunday clothes in the bureau drawer and thought of it along with Miss Pritchard's words in the classroom that day at recess. It comforted her when she got one of her spells of not being able to get words on paper.

8

THE FIRST three months of that second year of high school were the best Enie had ever known. She lived, moved and had her being in school; existence outside it was little more than an inconsequential dream. Under Miss Pritchard's guidance she read more books than she had ever expected to see this side of the magical Someday toward which she moved. Miss Pritchard made additions to the meager required reading for sophomore English, eliciting groans of protest from the majority of her students. But to Enie the extra reading was a privilege comparable to stolen play in her childhood.

She read while she ironed, the book—often one of Miss Pritchard's own, as the school library was scantily stocked—propped against the sugar bowl on the table beyond the ironing board. She read while she rocked Jenny to sleep on Saturdays after

dinner, and on Sundays while Papa took his week-
ly nap or walked beneath the trees in the yard.
Once in a while she even crept out of bed and
stealthily lighted the lamp she had sneaked into her
room earlier; but eventually Papa noticed that he
was having to buy more kerosene and caught up
with her. There was a scene following this unfortu-
nate occurrence and Enie dared not repeat the
offense. That, and the night Papa thrashed Leeroy
for failing to fill the woodbox, were the only times
Enie remembered that she hated Papa and felt a
recurring twinge of the old anxiety for her doomed
soul.

She was really learning now, acquiring knowledge she would never lose—learning in spite of
Tired Creek and no money and Papa. She thought
she could feel her mind growing, as she had sometimes thought, in the early days of adolescence, she
had felt her body growing. She knew she had
improved herself; she no longer had to think before
she spoke grammatically, or stop to correct in
embarrassment a word too hastily used. She no
longer had to dread contact with Mary Lee
Williams, for Mary Lee seemed as willing as she to
leave their inglorious past where it belonged. Enie
had always loved school; now it absorbed and
possessed her till even Mamma was sometimes
exasperated at her preoccupation.

"I declare, Enie, I've spoke to you the last I'm
going' to without I let you feel the flat of my hand!
What on earth's got into you to set you so moony?

95

Can't you see it's makin' up to rain and diapers on the line? Hustle out there and get 'em in before I lose my patience."

And though Enie's body leapt to do Mamma's bidding her mind remained apart, feeling, exploring, reaching out.

The weather itself was on Enie's side this fall, remaining mild through Christmas. "I know you'd ought to have a new coat," Mamma said, "but I can't see my way to it, crops bein' so poor after the drought. Cash money's mighty short . . ."

"No shorter than my old coat," Enie retorted, but her cheerful pertness only made Mamma smile.

But when the cold did come, it came to stay, bringing things of greater moment than a coat for Enie.

All the children had colds; there was no reason to think Sue Ann's was worse than the others'. Leeroy had to stay home from school with a mustard plaster on his chest and coughed rackingly through the long nights, and Jenny had two frightening bouts of croup, blue in the face till Mamma thrust an experienced finger down her throat and brought out the suffocating phelgm.

Sue Ann played around the house with one of Papa's handkerchiefs pinned to the bosom of her dress so she could keep track of it. She ate heartily and made Enie laugh, teaching Jenny to blow her nose. She wouldn't keep her shoes on, though, and Mamma was always scolding her for running about the drafty floors in her bare feet.

In the middle of the fourth day of her cold Sue Ann put her tin dishes in their shoe box, pushed it behind the stove and climbed into her cot bed. When Enie came from school, Sue Ann was asleep and Mamma was growing uneasy. Sue Ann's breath rattled, her cheeks looked like hard round apples, redder than usual. Mamma put a hand on her forehead. "She feels like she's got a fever, but no wonder, I reckon. All these little younguns are rotten with cold."

Sue Ann woke before dark, but when Mamma tried to tempt her with milk toast sprinkled with sugar, she turned away fretfully and fell asleep again. Enie undressed her without waking her, pulling the little flannel nightgown over the damp curls, smoothing the quilts and tucking them firmly under the cot pad.

The next day Mamma met Enie and Henry Jim at the door with a scared face. "Papa's gone to Vances' to phone for the doctor," she told them. "First time he's put foot outdoors since feeding, this morning. He's rocked Sue Ann the livelong day."

Fear brushed Enie's mind. Papa wouldn't have gone for the doctor if he had not been afraid himself. He believed strongly in home remedies and distrusted prescriptions only Mr. Williams, the pharmacist, could read. Dr. Helms came and left medicine for Sue Ann, said he would be back in the morning.

Enie and Henry Jim stayed home from school without being told to, and Enie was washing the breakfast dishes when Dr. Helms came. She stole to the door of Mamma's room and listened, but the doctor's words circled thickly in her head, making little sense. There was mention of the hospital, an oxygen tent, a nurse . . . "I don't want to move her," Dr. Helms said. "Not now, not in this weather."

Papa did not set foot outside the house. He sat in Mamma's room beside Sue Ann's cot, or in the rocker in front of the fire, holding Sue Ann in his arms when she fretted. Once, Enie, reading to Leeroy in the next room, heard Papa singing—not in his big, booming church voice, but gently, crooning a silly thing Mamma sang the babies to sleep with. "Froggy went acourtin' he did ride, m-m-m-hmph," Papa sang, and the chair rocker squeaked a plaintive accompaniment. "Froggy went acourtin' he did ride, A sword an' a pistol by his side, m-m-hmph."

Around noon the doctor came again. "I'd like to bring a trained nurse out from the hospital," he said. Papa agreed instantly in a hoarse voice, "Anything you say, Doc, anything . . ."

The nurse arrived and the children stared at her white uniform and smiled shyly when she smiled at them, but Enie felt a nameless terror mounting within her. She ran out of the house and down to the branch. She pushed the bare willow branches aside and crept, shivering, onto the damp rock. Her terror was no longer nameless; she knew that Sue Ann was about to die. But when she tried to form a prayer she could not get beyond "Our Father." The two words scraped over and over, making a sore little track in her mind. I don't pray enough, she thought. It doesn't come natural— maybe God isn't even listening because I'm so wicked, all wrapped up in myself, thinking I'm so smart and not caring about other people, not even my own folks. More frightened than ever, she went slowly to the house, her thin shoulders hunched against the wind that was blowing lead-colored clouds across the sky.

Sue Ann's illness did not cost very much money; it was all over so soon. The trained nurse shook her head and said to Dr. Helms, not knowing Enie stood behind her in the hall, "I wouldn't take a penny for this case. I couldn't. I only washed my hands once, never gave the little thing but one dose of sulfa . . . Why, it's not even dark yet . . ."

Enie looked toward the door. Dirty winter dusk showed through the knotholes in the wall. But for the awful sound of Mamma's choked sobbing and the measured pacing of Papa's feet in the front room, the house was still. Leeroy was asleep; Henry Jim had bolted to the barn when they told him; Jenny, unknowing, sat in the high chair that had been Sue Ann's a little while ago, eating her supper of bread and milk. Her tiny hand took the spoon carefully from the bowl to her lips, her big eyes intently watching Snowball at her evening bath.

Sue Ann is dead, Enie thought, and she made her lips form the words again and again, a dry whisper like the scrape of an oak leaf on hard ground. "Sue Ann has just died. *Sue Ann . . .*" ..

Enie stood in the hall, not knowing where to go or what to do. She dared not intrude upon the enormity of Mamma's grief. And Papa—his footsteps did not pause once. Enie shuddered, having no way to measure Papa's loss, thinking numbly, if it had been any one of us but Sue Ann, his darling, his pet . . . For a wild, grief-crazed instant she thought of going into the front room, of throwing her arms about Papa, of laying her head on his breast where it had never lain in all her memory but where Sue Ann's had often rested . . . But she couldn't do it, she did not dare. She trembled in the face of adult sorrow, knowing no way to touch it with her own. She stumbled to the door of her room, opened it and went in.

There was no fireplace in the room. Mean little drafts sneaked in round the windowpanes. Leeroy lay on Enie's bed under the quilts, asleep. His parted lips were cracked with fever. Enie saw the bones under the transparent delicacy of his peaked face, his forehead high and bony, his closed lids marked with blue veins like thin lines drawn in ink. How much more frail he looked than Sue Ann ever had! Yet it was Sue Ann who had been

stricken down. She lay in there in Mamma's room
. . . and she was dead.

Leeroy turned his head. His hair needed cutting—
it always did—and thrust upward in dark tufts
to hold up his head with all that ragged, heavy
hair. I haven't been close to Leeroy in such a long
time, Enie thought in anguish. I used to be—but
lately I haven't felt close to anybody at home.
Leeroy never tells me what he thinks about any
more, he never tells me lies any more . . . She felt
an urgent need to touch Leeroy, to seize and
hold him . . . But it wouldn't do any good. Papa's
strong arms had not been able to hold Sue Ann
from death. She stared at Leeroy till tears, crawling
down her cheeks, made her cover her face with her
hands.

Later, Mamma tried to quiet Enie's rebellious
storm of weeping. "The Lord giveth and the Lord
taketh away," she said in a trembling voice.
"Blessed be the name of the Lord." But Enie had
to grind her teeth together to keep from saying
something terrible in reply.

———————

All that first night and most of the following day
Papa walked back and forth, back and forth in the
front room, his measured tread falling like cudgels
on Enie's raw nerves. She thought dully that the
carpet Mamma had taken such care of since the
day it arrived from Sears Roebuck would surely be

threadbare from the constant crossing and recrossing.

There was no way to get word to T.H.—no one knew where he was—and the funeral took place without him, causing shocked whispers and headshakings. Leeroy, still coughing and unsteady on his spindly legs, was taken from his bed and dressed in his best. Aunt Pearl and Uncle Jud came from Andalusia, driving back that same night in the misting rain. And through it all Papa's face was like a piece of gray stone, unmoving but for the slow working of his teeth on his lip, a face more frightening in grief than it had ever been in anger.

All the rest of that winter, through the rain and cold that hung on dreadfully, Papa kept silent. Enie came to wish he would yell at somebody, strike out with his fists, do anything to show he was himself. But he scarcely seemed aware of them, lost and wandering as he was in his own bitter darkness. Only once he broke out, and that was at Mamma. He had come in from the lot and stumbled over the tin dishes scattered on the floor. He looked down and something like his old temper flamed into his face. "Put them things up," he commanded hoarsely. "Put 'em away, I say."

"I give 'em to the baby to play with," Mamma faltered, moving toward the toys.

"They was *hers,* wasn't they? Put 'em away where they belong to be. There's no need of 'em any more in this house."

Enie jumped ahead of Mamma, who had stopped as if she had lost her way in the middle of the room. She began gathering the tiny cups, the dented plates, thrusting them into the box Sue Ann had kept them in. When at last she dared look at Papa again, the last trace of his anger had faded, the stony look was back on his face. Enie took the box into the front room and put it with Sue Ann's clothes in the bottom bureau drawer.

The weeks dragged on with scarcely a good day. A cold wind drove gray sheets of rain before it, and Enie shuddered when she thought of the new grave at Pleasant Grove. She thought about God and heaven and hell a lot, too. She wondered if it was because she had no natural goodness in her that she could derive no consolation from the thought of her little sister "safe in the arms of Jesus," as they had sung at her funeral. Sue Ann didn't *know* Jesus; what if she was homesick, such a little girl so far away from home? Or—what if there was nothing at all to this business of everlasting life and Sue Ann was only a bit of clay now in the grave. At least, if that were so, nothing could make any difference to her.

School had lost its heady flavor; even Miss Pritchard seemed changed, Enie thought sometimes—as if her mind was not in the schoolroom. Just after Enie's return following the trouble, Miss Pritchard met her in the hall one day. "Remember what I said once, Earline, about life's being an important teacher?" Enie nodded, the lump in her throat preventing words. "It can be cruel, too, I know." She caught Enie's hand and pressed it between her palms, adding, "I was so sorry to hear . . ."

It was her schoolwork, now, that Enie did with a part of her mind; tragedy had wrenched her back into the family. She longed for spring but it held off, the rain winding Tired Creek in a drab curtain day after day. It was hard to believe there had ever been a time when the community with one accord prayed for rain. Lying in bed one night, listening to the fitful wind, she thought: I don't hate Papa now. You can't hate and pity at the same time. That's something I've learned from all this.

9

It came to an end at last, that winter. Spring flew her many flags, sweeter for their lateness. The drawn look in Mamma's face eased, little by little, and Papa took his sorrow into the fields where the steady harshness ground some of it away and laid a tough scar over what was left. Enie's compassion for him all too soon became a memory—less vivid, less enduring than the memory of Sue Ann or the happy, mind-enriching months before Sue Ann died.

Mamma still watched Mr. Orin Thompson's battered Ford approach the mailbox with anxious hope, but no letter came. "Sometimes," she said after one of these disappointments, "I feel better about Sue Ann than I do about T.H. I know she'll never know want or sorrow or sufferin', but T.H.—

I just have to try to give him into the dear Lord's hands."

"T.H. is all right, Mamma, for goodness' sakes," Enie said impatiently. "He's doing what he wants to, isn't he?" And she added, "I think he's pretty lucky, myself."

"Don't talk like that, Enie. Maybe he is and maybe he's not."

Gentled by Mamma's pain, Enie said then, "Try not to worry about him, Mamma. Children are bound to grow up and leave home." She put her finger on her tongue, tested the flatiron with a quick touch. "I'll go too, someday."

Miss Pritchard did not come back to Green Pine school that year. Such rumors as may have circulated in town did not reach Enie in Tired Creek, and it was with a violent shock that she saw another English teacher behind Miss Pritchard's desk on the first day of school.

The new teacher was a young man named Agnew. He had a round pink face and sandy hair already thinning, and a nervous smile that begged to please. He was under Mary Lee Williams' spell from the first bold flash of her dimples, but Enie was too stunned to care about that. It was Mary Lee who told her why Miss Pritchard had not returned.

"She got married to a man from up north.

Somebody she knew when she went to school up there." Mary Lee giggled, looking the way she did when a boy spoke to her. "I reckon she'll live in New York now."

All that first day Enie moved dazedly from one classroom to another, her throat aching with the need for a good cry. She was glad when three o'clock came and she could creep onto the bus, turning a deaf ear to the clatter about her. When she told Mamma, blurting the news when she was halfway up the walk, she could hold back no longer and abandoned herself to tears.

Mamma was at a loss to comfort her. She kept making murmuring sounds and shaking her head. "Well, I just declare," she said over and over. When she had let Enie cry herself to a degree of calm she said, "You want to be glad for her. It's meant a woman should marry and have children— without the Lord's got some other purpose for her."

"Just when I was getting to where I could write a little bit," Enie mourned.

"Maybe," Mamma offered cautiously, "you was comin' to depend on Miss Pritchard too much. Maybe it's for the best you have to stand on your own two feet with it now."

"But I didn't even know I wanted to *be* a writer till she showed me I did," Enie argued.

"It was there, don't you worry," Mamma affirmed. "She couldn't of seen it if it hadn't. She never give you the gift; the good Lord was the one did that, an' He'll see you get on with it, too, if it's the way for you. This might of been meant. God moves in mysterious ways His wonders to perform."

"Oh, Mamma, you're always saying that. Do you honestly believe it?"

There were other changes now, less personal and much more remote than Miss Pritchard's resignation, yet making themselves felt in Tired Creek, reaching across the ocean Enie had never seen, coloring the simple talk of the farmers squatting on their heels in Pleasant Grove churchyard on preaching Sundays. The ominous cloud which would shadow the world before long did not miss Tired Creek. Now and then a note of excitement pierced the gloom: If war came, they said, prices of farm produce would go high, higher than you could believe. Remember last time? Then it was Kaiser Bill and now it was Hitler, but the result was bound to be the same.

"It'll be just like us to stick our noses into what ain't our business, like we done before," Papa said angrily, flinging his paper to the floor. "If everybody was to tend to their own jobs like the good Lord meant 'em to, there wouldn't be no wars." But Mamma shook her head and said there would always be wars; didn't the Book say so? Wars and rumors of wars.

"Didn't you have a brother killed in the World War, Mamma?" Enie asked.

"Yes, I did. Your Uncle Thurston, one T.H. was named after." And Enie could see she was thinking that if there was another world war, T.H. and Henry Jim would be called to go.

And so it slipped into their talk, but as yet the business of scratching a living from their few acres was still the absorbing thing. For Enie there was the gigantic problem of an education pressing ever closer and her prospects growing no brighter. Without Miss Pritchard's faith and encouragement it was hard to believe in it at all, though she could no more relinquish it than she could forego drawing her breath.

———

Mamma was ailing from time to time that winter, claiming it was nothing but age catching up to her. She refused to see Dr. Helms and took baking soda for the "indigestion" that sometimes troubled her. One Saturday Enie caught her lying on the front room bed after dinner, and her uneasy questioning brought out Mamma's reluctant admission that an afternoon rest had become a habit with her.

"Reckon I'm getting lazy an no-'count like Doc," Mamma mocked herself. But Enie was troubled. She could not remember Mamma's ever having been either lazy or ailing.

10

ALREADY THE FIELDS were lush with the crops Papa had managed to put in with only the help of Henry Jim between school hours. The weather had been good all the time; school had been out for almost a month, and roasting ears, tomatoes, beans and black-eyed peas made good eating, while they furnished the needed brawn and energy for all the work that filled each day. It seemed to Enie she could hardly remember when Papa had last roared at anyone in a temper; he was worn out at the end of the hot day and usually rolled into bed as soon as he had swallowed his supper and sloshed the field dirt off his feet with cool water.

But that evening was especially close, and they were all out front to get any chance breeze that might be stirring. Mamma slumped in her rocker with Jenny in her lap; Papa and Henry Jim lay on the floor, bare soles turned to the sky; and Enie sat on the edge of the porch, dangling her legs. Leeroy, who had been darting crazily round the yard, a shadow among shadows, now lay spread-eagled in the sandy walk. In spite of the dull, steady aching in all her joints, Enie felt peaceful. A little lightheaded with fatigue, but not restless, not quiveringly expectant, not despairing. Just peaceful—as if she could sit here and breathe in the night scents and ever so faintly detect the promise of cooling dew forever.

It was at that moment that they heard somebody coming along the road, singing—a tune Enie had never heard and could never recall afterward—in a strong, clear tenor voice that belonged to nobody in Tired Creek.

Leeroy sprang up from the ground like a startled animal and froze into an attitude of listening.

"Who in tarnation's that, hollering like a mawkin' bird?" Papa complained sleepily. And then he sat up, for the singer came into view in the moonlit road opposite the gate. He looked to be about Henry Jim's height, but as slight as Henry Jim was solid. His shadow ran out, long and black, and the small shape of a bundle showed on his back as he bent over the latch.

"Wonder who it is," Mamma said, and as if he had heard, the singer stopped his song and hailed the house, country fashion, "Hello!"

Enie drew her dusty feet up and sat on them;

Henry Jim rolled to his side and leant on an elbow; Leeroy stood like a statue. The stranger called again, "Hello, folks!" And Papa returned a gruff "Howdy?" The plowshare that served as a weight clanked against its baling wire; the gate creaked open and the stranger came along the walk between the upended bottles. Seeing the figure pass Leeroy and draw near enough to reach out and touch her, Enie felt a strange pulsing start all over her like little hammers softly knocking. She couldn't tell what the face was like, though the figure was bathed in moonlight when it came out of the tree shadow and halted at the step. Old Minnie growled, then hunkered down and began to thump her scabby tail on the step.

"Didn't think to find anybody up—haven't seen a light for more than a mile," the visitor said in a slightly high, flattish voice. "Pretty near as dead back in town as it is out here."

Mamma remembered her manners and invited the stranger to have a seat. With a "Thank you kindly, ma'am," he dropped to the porch above the step and, taking the bundle from his back, set it between his feet.

"What might your name be?" Papa inquired. "Ourn's Singleton."

"Pleased to meet you, sir. Mine's Culpepper. Born Calhoun Darius but it was a little too much for me to ever catch up to, I reckon. Got shortened to C.D. and that got run together to make Seedy."

He touched Minnie's head and again her tail thumped frenziedly on the boards of the step.

"Whereabouts you bound fer?" Papa asked. He was squatting on his heels, now, wide-awake.

The stranger laughed. "I'd say that's up to you, sir."

"M-mm! How'd that be, now?"

The stranger felt in his pocket, cupped his hands about the match flame he had produced with a flick of his thumbnail, and drew hard on a cigarette. In the brief light his face showed for a second, thin and burnt bronze under a knobby forehead with a lock of sun-bleached hair across it. Enie, so near him, caught a tangy, wild-woods scent mingled with smoke.

"How's it up to me where you'd be going?" Papa demanded, irritated at the time it was taking the stranger to answer him.

"Well, it's a piece of luck finding you all up. Hope you won't take it wrong if I should ask for a night's lodging."

The cheek of him took Enie's breath. She dared not look around as Papa snapped, "What might your business be?"

Seedy Culpepper considered. "If you mean my trade—on the one hand, I have none; on the other . . . any number according to how you regard it, sir. Steady employment, no; that I have never had. I reached working size at the wrong time, or in the wrong world. Product of economic disaster and world chaos. I suppose I am a wanderer, to tell you the truth."

Leeroy had been inching nearer during the conversation. He stood less than a foot away from the visitor now, and Enie saw the harmonica's metal trim flash in the moonlight. She knew he was itching to try the tune that had come out of the night ahead of the stranger.

"If you mean what can I do to earn my keep, Mister," Seedy Culpepper went on when Papa said nothing, "that is a different matter. I can take aholt and do whatever needs doing. Officiated at an unexpected birthing a few weeks back—due partly to my experience as hired hand to a veterinary doctor but mostly to expediency . . ."

"No need to brag on yourself," Papa broke in.

"No bragging intended," Seedy said smoothly. "I don't carry written qualifications, I only state 'em when asked to."

"Where you from?"

"Well now, I was born in the state of Virginia. Western part of the state, close to the border of West Virginia. Town named Gate Forge. My old man worked a milk route. Could be I developed a fondness for the road joggin' around with him when I was a little shaver and never got over it. Anyway, I've stayed with the road, it being to my liking." He dropped his cigarette and placed his heel on the glowing end. He turned his head, quickly scanning the bright and shadow of the yard. "You got a nice place here, sir. Nice and neat."

"Do the best I can," Papa said. "Always short-handed. My farm is small, sixty acre. They call that a one-mule farm, but it hustles man an' mule to run it. My boy here, he's a good worker, but he goes to school an' that cuts into some busy times. Reckon you could say I make it an' that's about all." He spat into the yard.

"I helped a man up in Montgomery County, plowing time," Seedy Culpepper informed Papa. "Nights are still cool for sleeping out. He put me up for the help . . ." He let the sentence hang for Papa to get used to it.

"Hit ain't cool now by a long short," Papa observed.

Seedy Culpepper laughed. "Can't start an argument that way. But mosquitoes can be a considerable nuisance. I'm partial to outdoor sleepin' myself, but there comes times when a roof makes a nice change."

"That's what most humans figger," Papa said, pointedly.

Jenny whimpered and Mamma told Enie to take her in to bed. Enie reluctantly unfolded her legs. She didn't want to miss a word of the exchange between Papa and this boy—or man, she couldn't decide which. She lugged Jenny into the house and dumped her onto the bed, standing in a fever of impatience to see if she was going to settle down.

When she got back to the porch, Mamma was talking to the visitor. "How old are you, son?"

"Twenty years and four months, ma'am."

"Folks livin'?"

"My old man died two years ago. T.B. My mamma lives with my sister back up there in the mountains."

"Don't you never go back to see her?"

"I haven't been back since my dad cashed in."

"Hit must be hard on your ma—losin' you thisaway."

"Well, ma'am, me being there wouldn't necessarily mean she hadn't lost me. A man's got to go his route; anyhow I got to." His tongue gentled the harsh words. Papa gave a tearing yawn.

"Hit's gittin' late," he said, pointedly. "for folks that work for a livin'."

Enie squatted down by Mamma's chair. She saw the young man's head turn, felt his glance flick over her crouched body. Henry Jim had moved out to the yard, but Leeroy was on the step, close to the stranger. His profile stood out, sharp and birdlike, in the moonlight. Seedy Culpepper eased off the step and stood beside Henry Jim, facing Papa.

"I could help you with your work tomorrow, to pay for a night's lodging," he said. "I eat hearty—when I got it to eat, but I work the same way. I'd be much obliged to have the chance to prove it, sir."

Enie held her breath. In a moment the stranger would go or stay. She leaned forward, trying to see Papa's face, but it was in shadow. Silence stretched out maddeningly.

"I wasn't aimin' to take on ary hand," Papa said at last. "I could use a bean picker. It's backbreakin' work, but my wimmen folks have been helpin' at it."

"No need of that," Seedy Culpepper said promptly, not moving. "I'm a good bean picker."

"Mind you, I ain't able to pay cash wages."

"I'm asking bed and board. When I got to have cash, I guess I can make out to rastle it up." He moved then, touching Leeroy's head as he had touched Minnie's. Mamma's voice came out of the shadows, so unexpected it made Enie jump. "You hungry, son?"

"No, ma'am. I had my supper at the cafe in town."

"You got a place you can sleep him?" Papa asked Mamma.

"I reckon so," Mamma murmured, sounding worried and uncertain. Enie hadn't meant to butt in, but she heard herself asking with half-stifled eagerness, "Want me to make up the front room bed, Mamma?" and Mamma, still uncertain, said again, "I reckon so."

"Pump's in the back," Papa announced and got up to stretch till his finger tips touched the roof.

Backing toward the door, Enie saw Seedy Culpepper reach for his bundle and follow Henry

Jim to the back. Leeroy loped after them, pretending not to hear Mamma calling him.

Enie's hand jerked at the corners of the sheet. Culpepper. Calhoun Darius. C.D. Seedy Culpepper. A funny name. A funny boy—man. A wanderer. The word set her brain atingle. She wondered whereall he had been. All over the country, maybe! A boy could do that if he took a notion. Just take off and follow the roads. Big roads and little ones. It would be wonderful to do that—like T.H. and Seedy Culpepper. Forcing herself to be honest, she had to admit that his wanderings were but a part of what excited her; Seedy himself did— the nerve of him, the flashes of crude wisdom that lighted his speech, the unexpectedness of him.

She had finished with the bed and was about to leave the room when her eye lighted on the red glass dish containing Mamma's egg and preserve money. Maybe she ought to take it from the bureau and give it to Mamma . . . Then she was quickly ashamed. The wanderer wouldn't steal; she knew it. She took the lamp from the table and stood in the middle of the room a moment longer, seeing the fluted edge of the dish wink rosily. Then she walked out, taking the lamp with her. There would be moonlight for the stranger to see by, and she knew Papa would object to her leaving a lamp for someone who had strayed in like this.

He was standing just outside the door, Henry Jim behind him. One of Papa's shoes hit the floor in the other room. He was going to bed and to sleep

118

as if nothing out of the ordinary had happened, but Henry Jim's face was eager and curious. C.D. Culpepper looked at Enie with eyes bright and brown as a squirrel's. His nose tilted a little, giving impudence and gaiety to his face; the lock of bleached hair—yellow-white in the brown of the rest—swung between his eyes. His little bundle—a faded plain shirt wrapping other garments—hung from his hand.

"Can you make out without the lamp?" Enie asked bashfully.

Laughter danced to the surface of his eyes, crinkled over his too-thin face, making the planes of it all slant upward. "I generally make out by starlight—and there's a moon tonight." He glanced past her into the shadowy room with the rose-pattern art square on the floor and lace curtains at the window. The bed showed high and white. "It's a fine room I'm to sleep in, ma'am," he said, and Enie blushed at this teasing. "It'll come to no hurt through me, I promise you."

"Well, good night . . ." She steadied the lamp, feeling awkward and shy.

"Good night, ma'am," C.D. Culpepper said. "And thank you kindly. Hope I haven't made trouble."

Enie brushed quickly past him with lowered eyes, seized the brown china knob and closed the door on a creak of little-used hinges. She and Henry Jim looked at each other.

"How long you reckon he's going to stay?" Henry Jim whispered loudly.

"Long enough to work out his keep, I guess," Enie whispered back.

"You younguns git that light out and git to bed," Papa called in a voice muted by drowsiness.

11

THE EVENING of the first day came and Seedy Culpepper did not go. A week went by and Enie changed the sheets on the front room bed, washed and ironed Seedy's second set of work clothes. Mamma mended the rent in his shirt and reinforced with sturdy patches the seat and knees of his threadbare jeans. Preaching Sunday came and Seedy put on his third—and best—shirt and his faded cotton pants and went to church. After that, Enie noticed that Mamma lost her uneasiness and a certain wariness she had maintained toward the stranger who had come into their midst. Enie thought the vacant spot T.H.'s going had left in Mamma seemed filled, or at least its aching eased by her motherly care of Seedy.

"You reckon he's going to live with us, Mamma?" Enie asked, hiding the hope that trembled through her. "Papa doesn't mind a bit, does he?"

Indeed, Papa's eye had these days a glint of complacency at the good luck that had befallen him who had ever been the child of ill fortune. He stood only to gain, for he paid Seedy no cash wages, and victuals were plentiful. The only cost was the women's work of preparing it and the slightly heavier washing—and that was no concern of Papa's.

"I don't know what to make of it," Mamma said at last in answer to Enie's question. "Could be, he's tired of traipsin' the roads an' craves a spell of settled life like other folks. Anyhow, he's in no way beholden to us, all the help he is to your pa and Henry Jim. I don't hardly know what they'll do when he goes."

"Maybe he aims to stay till harvest is over," Enie thought aloud, feeling that with school to occupy her she might be able to face Seedy Culpepper's going.

When Ralph Shane rode past the house, Enie no longer hurried to the porch that he might wave to her; she hardly thought of the Shanes at all, telling Seedy of them and the way they lived with a brevity that was almost impatient. It was far more gratifying to sit on the porch in the early evenings and hear Seedy playing Leeroy's harmonica and telling his incredible, yet irresistible tales. There were nights, though, when Seedy washed and changed his clothes and went off toward town, striding along the road, whistling, as if he were not bone-weary from a day in the blistering field. Aside from reminding them that Seedy was a hobo, Papa made no comment on these expeditions, but sometimes fear touched Enie as she watched him go. What if he shouldn't come back and slip soundlessly into the front room in the small hours when the house was deep in sleep? What did he do those nights in Green Pine? How did he come by the cash money he sometimes jingled in his pockets? Money for his cigarettes and the candy and chewing gum he gaily dropped into Leeroy's and Jenny's outstretched hands.

He told her, one day, without shame or pretense. He said he won it, playing pool in the room back of Hudson's hot dog stand. Enie was properly horrified. "If Papa was ever to find out . . ." She shivered while Seedy grinned.

"Bet he'd kick me out right on my ear, wouldn't he?"

"He sure would. He's awful set against gambling. So is Mamma. You know what a good church member she is!"

"Well, they're not liable to find out, are they? If your old man was to ask me where I get my change, I'd tell him just like I told you. But what's he care as long as I keep my end of the deal we made? Don't fret your pretty little head, honey. I can take care of C.D. Culpepper; hasn't anybody else had it to do since I could scrounge around for him."

He tossed the bleached lock of hair out of his face. Enie was pink with embarassment because it was the first time a boy had ever called her "honey." She'd heard Papa say once that Seedy Culpepper had gall enough for anything, and she knew it was so.

Sometimes, lying awake at night, thinking of Seedy, Enie was afraid of the way she felt—weak and dazed, and those little hammers knocking all over her, soft and blunt, under her skin. But even her fear was sweet and not to be relinquished. She did not write a word the whole time Seedy was there, and when they were together it was Seedy who talked and Enie who listened, interrupting only occasionally to question him, breathlessly. She could not hear enough of the things he had seen— mountains in whose shadow he had been born and knew like the back of his hand, snow he had seen and touched and nearly frozen his feet in more than once, the ocean whose surf had crashed upon his hearing, the cities he had passed through and briefly tarried in.

"Did you ever see New York?" Enie breathed.

"Sure. That was the first place I hit out for when I left home. Hitched rides all the way." He shook his head. "I reckon, when you come right down to it, I don't have much hankering for cities. Seems like folks are in too much of a hurry. Pushing, tromping over one another to get where they're going. You never seen anything like it, Enie!"

"I only wish I could," Enie told him, hugging

her knees and rocking back and forth. "I know somebody living in New York City right now. She was my teacher. My friend, too."

Seedy chuckled. "That'd be the day, when I had a teacher that was my friend! You're a funny little critter, you are." He cocked the eyebrow that had a small white scar beneath it. "What would you call me, now—a friend?"

"Well, aren't you my friend?"

"You couldn't bring yourself to say 'boy-friend,' I reckon?" Enie saw his eyes, dancing with laughter, fixed on some point in the red road. She did not bother to answer him; he was just deviling her, of course.

One night he seized the opportunity to speak to her while she stood at the water bucket on the back porch. "How about going to the show tonight?" he asked, standing so close she could feel his breath on her cheek.

"How'd we get to town—walk?" She made her tone light and pert, but her eyes shone at the thought of going to a picture show with Seedy. It would be a real, honest-to-goodness date with him, like having him court her. Suddenly she longed beyond all reason to go to the Palace Theater in Green Pine with Seedy Culpepper.

"If Henry Jim went along, your old man might let us take the pickup."

"He won't," Enie sighed. "You know he won't. Better not even ask him." She was always afraid

Seedy would antagonize Papa and send the beautiful summer up in a blazing row.

"I got a plan," he said, glancing toward the kitchen door.

"Even if we got there," Enie went on, "It costs thirty cents apiece . . ." But Seedy pinched her arm, making goose-pimples spring out, warm as the evening was. "I'm in the dough. When you going to quit worrying about me and my money?"

Enie drew her palms elaborately along the sweaty sides of the bucket. "What kind of a plan?"

"You wait and see." He touched her arm lightly, as if he hardly thought about what he was doing, but Enie closed her eyes against the flutter beneath her breast. Seedy went into the kitchen and she heard him teasing Mamma, making her laugh. When she took the pitcher of water in to Mamma, Seedy was clearing the table, whistling under his breath.

When Mamma asked in a casual, offhand tone if the younguns could ride into town to the picture show, Papa looked at her as if she'd gone out of her mind, then scratched his head, frowned at his feet, and chewed down on his toothpick. Enie held her breath, the clock ticked loud enough to scare you, and Mamma added, "I wouldn't be in favor of night gadding myself, often, Clement. I reckon you know that. But all these young ones has worked hard today. A little treat can't do 'em any harm."

Enie waited for Papa to say it would cost too

much, and that would bring up the subject of Seedy's treating them, which might set Papa to wondering where Seedy got his spending money. She saw now that Seedy's plan had been to put Mamma up to asking Papa, as if the idea were all her own; it looked as if Papa had fallen for it hook, line and sinker, but surely he would balk at money spent on tomfoolery like that . . .

"You all be back here by ten o'clock," Papa said then, making Enie jump. "One minute late, an' you'll see no more shows in Green Pine or anywheres else." He reached his pipe from the shelf and headed for the front porch.

Enie let out her breath and raised her eyes to see Henry Jim and Seedy bent double in soundless mirth. She felt laughter rising in herself, filling her throat, brimming to her lips and eyes. She fled to her room to put her best dress on, all thumbs in her haste. Seedy had put a spell on them all, she thought. Even Papa.

———

After the night of the picture show Enie knew that Seedy was courting her. He was as wary as she, knowing what the cost of raising Papa's suspicions would be. But sometimes, when Papa had gone to bed as soon as he ate and Mamma was forced by her plaguing weakness to follow—so weary she sometimes forgot to send Enie to bed, too—Enie and Seedy and Henry Jim would sit on the porch,

Seedy spinning his yarns for the entertainment of the other two.

After a while Seedy would get up and stretch and say he felt like a walk. "Go with me, Enie?" he would say. Henry Jim never tagged along. He would stay stretched on the floor as if he hadn't heard, and Enie would follow Seedy to the gate, thrilling to the way he held it open for her to pass through and out onto the road.

One night, under the big oak that was their point of return, Seedy put his arms around her. Enie felt fear then, distant and hardly strong enough to make her draw back, but fear like a voice warning her—weakly and far away. She felt a quick anger at the voice, but the anger was lost as Seedy kissed her without any adolescent blundering; Seedy's lips were as wise as Enie's were ignorant. He kissed her gently, and her fear dissolved. She wanted the strong, tough arms tight around her in the insect-shrilling night, the kiss that burst like a star in her mind, in her body.

The headlights of the car and the smooth throbbing of its motor broke rudely into her ecstasy, tearing her from Seedy's arms. They stood trembling and watched the car go past. "One of those darn Shanes," Seedy remarked.

"We got to go back to the house," Enie said shakily. "Mamma might miss me."

"Mamma might miss me," Seedy mimicked, but not unkindly. "When you going to grow up, kid?

128

Anybody'd think this was the first time you ever got kissed by a feller."

"It was," Enie admitted humbly.

"Sweet sixteen and never been kissed. Well, you have now and I reckon that makes you my girl, don't it?"

"Do you want me to be your girl?"

"Yeah. I didn't at first; I don't like strings on me, see? You go and get tangled up with a girl . . . Well, I just didn't aim to do any such thing. But I don't know, there's something about you that gets me. Your red hair maybe." He put his hands on her hair. "How about another kiss before I take you home to your mamma?"

Enie didn't mind his laughing at her now. The happiness in her was almost more than she could contain. Seedy Culpepper wanted her for his girl! She hadn't flirted with him; she didn't know how. It was something you had or didn't have, a gift— and she didn't have it. She had just been here, a girl, quiet and listening, and her heart wide open to him.

Henry Jim was not on the porch when they got to the house, and the reassuring sound of Papa's snoring drifted out the front door. Seedy gave Enie's arm a little pinch and vanished round the corner of the house. Enie took off her shoes and tiptoed through the hall and into the room. She lay a long time, listening to the night sounds—insects churring as though the heat gave them as much energy as it sapped from humans, a tentative note from a mockingbird followed by a peal of song, pure and glittering as spring water, a choked cry from the boys' room where Leeroy must be having a bad dream. She wondered if Seedy were lying awake, too. She had not heard him come in; nobody ever heard Seedy come in.

August, hot and thundershowery, was upon her before Enie could believe it. School seemed remote in spite of its imminence; she had entered another world and was unwilling to share its wonders with thoughts of that which had once been dear. Papa set the boys at chores about the lot and yard. They put wire round the chicken run and hauled boards from Howells' sawmill for the lot fence T.H. had not properly repaired. Papa talked of new flooring for the shed loft, but did not get to it. Ordinarily these jobs would have had to wait for winter's leisure, but Enie knew Papa was taking advantage of Seedy Culpepper's clever hands. Harvest time was not far away, and the slack time would follow when he would no longer need Seedy's help so much. Would Seedy take his little bundle and go?

Mamma took Jenny and rode with Miss Sadie Hightower to visit with Mrs. Vance the day the lot fence was finished. After a short rest Henry Jim went off to the potato field where Papa was hoeing. Seedy remained on the back step, smoking a cigarette. Enie put aside the skirt she was letting the hem out of and went to the washstand to splash water over her hot face. The house was so still, the buzzing of a fly sounded loud against the pane. It had not rained and the afternoon was sultry and close. Enie knew she ought to have the skirt done by the time Mamma got home, but it was so hot—she was only going to cool off a little. She went out and sat down beside Seedy.

"How's it look?" Seedy demanded, jerking his head toward the fence.

"Fine. You all worked fast, too. You always work fast, don't you, Seedy?"

Seedy's eyebrow shot up. "Not always, I don't. Some of my work around here's gone mighty slow."

Enie felt the red coming up in her face. Seedy went on, coaxingly, "How come we don't take us a walk, now we have the opportunity?"

"I've got some sewing I'm supposed to get done," Enie began weakly, but Seedy grabbed her hand and pulled her up from the step.

"Sewing! You can sew when I'm in the field, can't you?" When he stood up, the muscles rippled under his bronzed skin. Enie's look crept, unbidden, to the sodden heap of his shirt on the end of the step.

"Where would we go? It's so hot . . ." She didn't know why she was trying to find excuses when she wanted so badly to go with Seedy. Anywhere, it didn't matter. She couldn't seem to take her eyes from the damp ball of his shirt.

"I know a place as cool as anything," Seedy said. "Down by the branch. Come on, I'll show you. Watching water makes you think you're cooler even if you're not." He reached down for his shirt and slipped it on.

They picked their way along the half grown over path through the dog fennel to the edge of the piny woods and followed the branch. At the screen of willows Seedy stopped and parted the drooping limbs. He looked so pleased with himself, Enie had to laugh.

"I've been knowing about this place all my life," she explained. "I used to come here a lot." She was shocked to realize how long it had been since she had sought the spot for solitude in which to write.

"By yourself?"

She nodded. "I came to *be* by myself."

Seedy pushed her gently through the opening and crawled in after her onto the flat rock. "Ain't it better like this?" he asked softly.

"I—I— don't know," Enie faltered. She had, all at once, a feeling of betraying something precious. Also, her heart had begun to knock in a frightened way. A change had come over Seedy with the softening of his voice. When she looked at him, shyly, she saw his eyes darker and holding something that burned and quivered like a flame. He touched her and she felt him trembling as she was.

"Enie honey, oh, Enie honey, I love you. Aw, little redheaded Enie, you don't want to be scared of me, sugar. You trust me, don't you?"

"I—I'm not scared of you, Seedy. I—I trust you, but . . . ."

"You love me, too don't you?"

"Yes! Oh yes, Seedy, I do love you, I do. But . . .

Through sudden tears she saw the pale green leaves of the willows; through a rushing in her ears she heard the faint splash of water falling over the little stones. Seedy held her so tightly she could not breathe, his arms asserting their superior strength. A picture flashed upon her confused and drowning mind—two pictures out of the past she had ignored and almost forgotten these last months: the first, herself, here on this rock hunched over her composition book, writing words that were to make her life and her world; the second, a tunnel of honeysuckle vines and Ralph Shane inside it with Bliss Atkins.

She was scrambling up, pushing at Seedy, thrusting him from her. The willows scratched her shoulder and neck, tore her dress as she pushed through them. She stood a moment at the edge of the stream agitatedly brushing at her clothes, pushing her hair out of her face. A moment more and she couldn't have torn herself away from Seedy.

He was standing beside her then, his face white, a muscle twitching at the corner of his mouth.

"You said you loved me," he accused her bitterly. "And I believed you. Well, you don't. You don't know anything about loving." His voice rose thinly. "This wasn't going to be any fly-by-night stuff. Not to me it wasn't! I wouldn't do it for anybody else. But you—for you I'd settle down. I'd marry you in a minute if there was need—you know—if anything happened to you on account of me—in there on the rock."

The color was coming back into his face; he touched her arm and when she did not move, his fingers closed about it, hurting a little but dear to her, too. "I could fix up a deal with your old man—just like I did at first, only for keeps this time. You know I could! Stay on and work this farm with him. Lord God A'mighty! I never figgered on getting trapped by a skinny little redhead like you, Enie, but I'd do it. For you, I would do it."

"Marry? You and me—marry? And live here at Tired Creek the rest of my days? Never set eyes on any other place? No, Seedy, no!"

She was crying now, jerking her arm from his grasp, wiping her eyes with her sleeve, walking away, stumbling, the mud sucking at her feet as if to hold her so her body would betray her after all. "I cannot stay here in Tired Creek." She was almost running now, gasping words at Seedy's steps coming heavily behind her. "And I don't want to get married—I've got plans—I know, I never told you. I couldn't—I was all mixed up after you came . . ."

In the clearing she slowed down, wiped her face again, smoothed at her hair and went on, not daring to look back. Maybe it was too late now ever to make Seedy understand about her hopes and dreams, but she couldn't help that. She must make sure of her escape.

When the house came into view, she looked back. Seedy was standing in the patch, slashing furiously at a clump of dog fennel with his pocketknife. She watched his form grow blurred and wavering through tears, whispered his name to herself. "Seedy . . . Seedy . . ."

12

AFTER SUPPER Papa went out to look at the new fence and Enie, getting at the dishes in a frenzy of energy, heard Seedy go along the hall and into the front room. She only half listened to Mamma's animated account of her afternoon with Mrs. Vance, and when she had finished with the dishes she slipped away to her own room to think. Standing in the dusky light of the room, twisting her hands together, she heard the screen door close—gently, not with its usual sharp slap—and knew as well as if she saw him that it was Seedy leaving the house.

Enie longed to rush out after Seedy, tell him she was sorry she had used him badly, tell him she hadn't meant to, explain fully all she had never told him till this afternoon when they were both beside themselves with desire and fear and anger. Tomorrow she'd manage to talk to him, she could not go running after him now with dark falling; Papa would be sure to miss her and there'd be a row, making everything worse than ever.

"Enie?" Leeroy's voice coming out of the shadows startled a little cry out of her. The shuck mattress rattled as he turned over.

"What are you doing in my room, Leeroy Singleton? You like to scared me to death."

"I ain't doin' nothing," Leeroy said, husky with drowsiness. "I was jus' layin' here an' I must of dropped off. I had me a dream—wanta hear it, Enie?"

"No." Enie felt unreasoning anger toward Leeroy. "No, I don't want to hear any dream. You go on to bed."

Leeroy rolled out and padded across the room. "I wisht I could make me a pallet out in the yard," he sighed as he went slowly through the door. "That was sure some dream—all about stars . . ."

Stars. Seedy had told them so many tales about sleeping under the stars. He said that if you looked at them long enough they got to be like old friends—always there, no matter where you were. Once, when Mamma wasn't present to accuse him of irreverence, he said he believed the stars were the face of God multiplied a billion times.

Enie groped blindly to the bed and fell across it. The warmth Leeroy's body had left seemed to flow through her skin as she smothered her wild sobs into the limp, musty pillow. When she woke from the exhausted sleep she had cried herself into, dawn was graying her window. Her lids felt heavy and her head ached. Her rumpled, sweaty clothing bunched uncomfortably under her and dulled thoughts fumbled after something. As she turned and sat up, the something jumped at her as if it had been waiting all the time to catch her.

She crept from her room and made her way in the dingy twilight through the hall. The front room door stood open. Folding her arms tight about her chest as though she must hold the pain inside it, she stepped into the room. It was empty, neat and tidy as she had left it yesterday; the bed had not been slept in. Enie crossed soundlessly to the wardrobe and looked in. Seedy's few shabby garments were gone—into the night, out of their lives.

Papa ranted and raved at Seedy's disappearance, saying he knew it would happen and what better could you expect of a hobo. But Mamma spoke up courageously to remind Papa that Seedy was not beholden to them; it was the other way round if anything. Jenny cried and Leeroy was silent with his far-off look, stealing away to the barn to play sad strains on his harmonica. Enie tried to make herself small, afraid to look at anyone lest her secret knowledge show. Now and then she caught Mamma eyeing her uneasily, but no words passed between them on the subject; Enie had a feeling that Mamma tactfully refrained from questioning her. But one evening when Enie was milking Bessie, Henry Jim loomed suddenly beside her.

"You sent him off," he broke out bitterly. "He was sweet on you—and you had a row with him."

Bessie kicked out nervously at the sudden jerk of Enie's fingers and the milk sloshed against the rim of the bucket. "I didn't want him to go," Enie said sullenly. "You know he was bound to—sometime. He belongs to the road." But her heart denied the cool matter-of-factness of the words.

She wandered for days in a maze of broken and trailing ends, feeling both aching and dead—the part of her that did not ache with dreadful persistence being numb and uncaring. The days ran into weeks and she knew now why they called it lovesickness, for the whole thing was like an illness that crept toward a slow convalescence shot with moments of relapse. School's opening did not shake her out of it, and the countryside was bleak and brown with winter before she recovered from her romance with Seedy Culpepper. Not till then could she think of it with calm and acceptance; not the spiritual acceptance Mamma displayed toward all adversity, but the knowledge of an experience over and done with.

———————

Mr. Claye, the school principal, stopped Enie in the hall one day and asked her if she expected to go to college. "Your record is extremely good, Earline. In fact, I might as well tell you, you stand a very good chance of being valedictorian of your class." The first tingle of excitement Enie had felt in months brought the color to her face. "I hope you intend to go to college?" His blue eyes shone piercingly behind the thick-lensed glasses he wore. "It would be a pity to halt such splendid progress."

Enie swallowed nervously. "I want to go to college," she said, "but I don't know—yet—if I can."

"Well, there's time, and where there's a will . . ." The principal smiled kindly and moved off down the hall.

Enie was preoccupied through her next class, and before she boarded the school bus she resolved to ask Papa point-blank whether there was any possibility of his sending her to Mills College next year.

That night, after the dishes had been put away and Papa had finished looking over the Green Pine Messenger, Enie faced him. He had put out a hand to turn the lamp down, but at Enie's first words, blurted suddenly in spite of all her previous determination to be careful and tactful, he let his hand fall to the table without even lowering the wick.

"Mr. Claye wanted to know if I'm going to college, Papa." She lowered herself to the edge of a chair and kept her gaze steadfastly on Papa's face.

Papa had eaten a good supper—sausage from yesterday's butchering and his favorite fig preserves. The frayed end of his toothpick was still between his lips. As Enie gazed at him, the color began rising in his face, his lids seemed to thicken, narrowing his eyes to strips of hot bright blue.

"What's it to Claye what you do when you get through his school?" There was a quiet about him that increased Enie's nervousness, a sort of weather-breeder mildness.

"I don't know, Papa, he's just interested in his students, I guess."

"M-mm." Papa's hand explored his stubbled chin. Enie could hear the scrape of whiskers against his finger. Jenny's chatter had stopped abruptly in the next room and Enie knew Mamma was listening. "Reckon he expects a man to say right out whether he can put money he hasn't got into gettin' a gal's head crammed with notions when it's already chockablock with 'em. Has been ever since that uppity teacher was here. Well, I don't aim to oblige him. You can tell him so if you want." He leaned toward Enie, his hair bristling almost against the lamp chimney. But still he had not raised his voice.

"Mills College doesn't cost so very much," Enie faltered, wanting to speak out bold and sharp, but unable to do so with Papa's face so close, his words echoing in her head. "It's the cheapest I could go to . . ."

"Cheapest." Papa bit the word in two, his

mouth twisting with the taste of it. "No school's cheap! Look what it cost me right here in Green Pine school. Taxes and this an' that, somethin' extry ever time you turn around. What about this graduation comin' along with all the tomfoolery that goes with it? I'll be lucky if I can scrape together enough for that, let alone another bait of schoolin'." He ran his hands through his hair till it sprang up like a brush fire.

"I didn't say it was cheap. But lots of colleges cost a lot more—most do—and it would be worth it if I could . . ."

Papa exploded, his voice loud enough now. "Worth it? It might be worth it if I had as much land as Tom Shane's got. But I haven't got it an' I ain't likely to get it. All I got's a gal with notions like a Shane. First your brother lights out soon's I got a right to look for some help from him, an' now you talk about bein' a burden on me—a strong, healthy girl like you that's already had a heap more schooling than any of her folks. Still, I notice we make out, even if we haven't got no fine college degrees to hang on the walls."

Anger cracked like a whip across Enie's nerves. She wanted to strike out at Papa, to send the lamp crashing from the table, to hurt him terribly, as he had hurt her. She felt her fury bearing down on her, clutching her like a wild thing in a trap.

"That will do, Clement," Mamma said from the doorway. Her eyes burned dark and hollow in her worn face. "You know good and well Enie's wanted to plan on goin' to college a mighty long time. It's not to get outa doing her part, neither. Earline has always done her part here at home. The more education anybody's got, the better job they can get, and who would she go to for help but her own blood pa?"

Jenny sidled up to Mamma and grabbed a fold of her nightgown, and Mamma's hand touched the silky head, her eyes not moving from Papa's subdued and sullen face. "You shame me, Clem Singleton, me and all your young ones, makin' a to-do over your daughter comin' to you like she has."

In silence Papa chewed his lip, looking neither at Mamma nor Enie. The color ebbed slowly from his face, leaving it sallow and bleak—as if his anger had been all he had to hide behind. He moved his hands toward the lamp, drew them back, looked at them.

"I could pay you back," Enie said. "I could pay back every cent—after I teach a while."

Papa raised his hands and brought them heavily to his knees. 'Can't you see it ain't there? I can't give or loan you what I've not got. I will not borry and have debt ridin' me for this or any other thing short of life or death."

Mamma's hand slid from Jenny's head.

"Go to bed, Enie," she said. "You best come too, Clem. Hit's been a hard day."

Enie got up stiffly. One of her feet had gone to sleep and she stumbled. She sat on the side of her bed, unaware of the chill in her fireless room. She heard Papa blow the lamp out gustily and clump out of the kitchen. After a time she heard the thump of his shoes on the floor, then the noisy clearing of his throat followed by one obdurate sentence: "I don't aim to borry unless there's sickness or the hand of the Lord is laid on me."

"How do you know this ain't the hand of the Lord?"

"Don't mock the Lord, Elnora."

"I'm not." Mamma's voice came through the wall. "I just don't see how you can be so certain-sure. The Lord moves in mysterious ways His . . ."

"Keep quiet, woman," Papa snarled.

Enie got up and began to undress. She felt the cold then, and kept shivering after she was in bed with the quilts drawn up to her chin. After a while she heard Papa begin to snore. A creak of the floor boards startled her; Mamma's hand touched her shoulder. Enie sat up.

"Lay down, honey," Mamma whispered. 'You're liable to catch cold. It's blowin' off mighty chilly."

"You'll take cold yourself," Enie whispered back. It came to her that they always talked of little things when big things lay on their hearts.

Mamma sat on the bed and folded her arms across her breast. "Your papa don't mean it. All that carryin' on's just pure bluff. He don't hold with too much education, I know that's a fact. But all that hardness—he just purely don't mean it."

An ache, faint and dull to begin with, swelling rapidly to anguish, would not let her answer Mamma or touch her, though she longed to lay her head in Mamma's lap and cry her misery away.

"Papa don't know anything," Mamma said sadly, "but fight and struggle. You got to fight too, Enie, your own way. You got a better chance than me or Papa . . ."

"What chance have I got?" Enie demanded bitterly.

"You got your youth and your good health. And you got time, that's the main thing, time. There's the rest of this school year an' the summer after. A way might come. You've got no call to give up hope—like somebody old." Mamma gave Enie a little push. "Scrooch over. I got my feet froze, settin' here in this draught."

Enie moved over against the wall and Mamma crept beneath the covers. She drew Enie's head against her shoulder. "Don't you never give up. It'll look different when day comes. Make the most of every school day you got left—there's many a one, yet."

But it did not look different to Enie when day came, nor for many days. The old hatred she had felt for Papa renewed itself till, at times, it was a pain in her vitals. At other times she drew a morbid sort of comfort from it; she'd show Papa, she'd get where she was going in spite of him, she'd show everybody. She had no faith in Mamma's predicted "way" that would be provided, but she'd make a way herself, somehow. Her old sense of guilt seemed as dead as the hope of Papa sending her to college till, with Papa's accident, it rose and smacked her full in the face.

13

IT WAS JUST before Christmas holidays and Enie was setting the table for supper. On her way to the safe for the butter she looked out the window and saw Papa come through the gathering dusk and disappear into the shed. A rasp of splintering wood followed, and Henry Jim came tearing out of the shed. The bucket dropped from his hand and milk flowed over the ground.

"Ma!" Henry Jim yelled, "Ma! It's Pa! He fell out of the loft!"

Mamma clutched at the bosom of her dress and made for the door, Enie at her heels. "Pa fell out of the loft and he's laying there like he's dead," Henry Jim was shouting at them as if they were deaf.

Enie peered over Mamma's shoulder into the near-dusk of the shed. Henry Jim was blubbering at her elbow, "I tried to get him to let me and Seedy put a new floor up there when we we done that buildin', last summer."

Mamma was on her knees beside Papa's motionless form. One leg was doubled under him, his eyes were not quite closed and a slow ooze of blood made its way from a corner of his mouth. Papa is dead, Enie thought, calm and clearheaded. I hated him so hard he's been killed. What is going to happen to us now? And she moved into the shed and squatted beside Mamma. I've mocked God, I reckon—and He will not be mocked.

Mamma's hand was moving across Papa's chest. She said, not turning her head, "You git in the truck, son, and go to the Vances'. Get 'em to phone for Dr. Helms, make haste! Papa's heart's goin'—but he's hurt bad, I reckon. Get Mr. Vance to come back with you an' help us get him to the house. Enie, you run get the bed ready in the front room—be quick, now."

The sheets she had put on the bed after Seedy left emitted a faintly damp smell. Enie ran her hands over them; they would have to do, no chance to change or air them now. She did take time to light a lamp and take it out to the shed. Mamma was still on her knees, rubbing Papa's hands, trying to talk to him. Leeroy and Jenny crowded in and began to cry. By the time Enie got them into the house and pacified them with sausage and biscuits she heard the clatter of the pickup truck in the yard. When she reached the shed door again she saw, in the lamplight, not Mr. Vance but Ralph Shane. Henry Jim was telling Mamma he'd been lucky enough to meet Shanes' car and Mr. Tom had gone home to telephone the doctor.

"How about getting the cow out of here?" Ralph suggested, and for the first time Enie was aware of Bessie, stolidly champing the hay Papa had thrown down as the floor gave way under him. Undisturbed by the commotion in the shed, she stood about three feet away from the groaning bulk of Papa. Henry Jim began to push and pull at the cow, sent her bawling out of the shed with a series of smacks on her bony rump.

Enie drew Mamma to her feet and took the lamp, holding it for Ralph, who now got down beside Papa, touching him carefully. "It's his leg— looks like it's broken." He tried to draw the leg from under Papa, but the rattling groans increased alarmingly and Ralph shook his head. "Better cover him up and wait for the doctor."

Enie gave the lamp to Henry Jim and ran in for quilts, stopping a moment to warm them at the stove. "Put some more wood in," she told Leeroy instead of answering the question he asked. "And stay right here with Jenny. Hear? You can have some pie if you'll cut it and give Jenny a piece."

As she helped Ralph Shane wrap the quilts about Papa, Mr. Tom Shane's car came up behind the truck, and Mr. Tom joined Ralph at Papa's side. Mamma began to cry, her face pale and twisted in the lamplight. It was quite dark now.

Outside, a wind had risen to rattle the oak leaves and sigh in the cracks of the shed. Rotten, splintered bits of wood lay under and about Papa.

Mr. Shane said, "Dr. Helms is on his way. It won't take long, the way he drives."

Leeroy's nerves had cracked under the strain of being shut out from the scene of activities, and he and Jenny were on the back porch howling at the top of their lungs when Dr. Helms careened into the yard. Papa looked up at the doctor and fainted dead away.

"Just as well," Dr. Helms observed. "He won't feel what I'm fixing to do to him."

———————

Papa had no internal injuries. He had knocked one tooth out, which he must have swallowed, for it never showed up, though Leeroy searched the ground carefully; and his right leg was broken in two places. Mamma kept saying it could have been worse, but this only enraged Papa.

"Yeah, it could of been worse," he mimicked, thrashing his arms and turning his head from side to side till Enie wondered how long the pillow slip would last. "I coulda broke my neck instid of my leg. I could of been layin' six foot under ground now, instid of in this durned bed, thinkin' about everythin' goin' to pieces an' wonderin' how I'm goin' to pay all the bills."

But Mamma refused to be ruffled. "That's what

I mean, Clem. You could of had to stay in the hospital; Dr. Helms thought you might have to when he first looked at your leg. But he got the cast on an' here you are at home. An' it could of happened in the spring—planting time or harvest. As it is, you got a good chance to mend fore there's much to do on the place. This is the best time it could come if it had to be."

But Papa went on thrashing and complaining bitterly of the malign fate that had attacked him. Dr. Helms said he must wear the cast at least six weeks; after that—they'd have to see. It might be he would sustain a slight limp, but not enough to make a cripple of him.

Enie could not recall ever having seen Papa in bed in the daytime. He was difficult about everything. Miss Sadie Hightower brought him a pair of crutches Sam Howells had used for months after a rattler bit him, and she stood by, aiding and abetting while Papa got the hand of using them. Through the holidays he thumped and shuffled, grunting, about the house, making Enie as nervous as a witch when he stood hunched between the crutches staring darkly at—or through—her. She couldn't shake off the guilt that made her feel responsible for Papa's accident—a thing she had brought upon him by hating him with such a vengeance—and was humbly grateful that she need not go through life with his death upon her soul.

"I hate to be beholden to Tom Shane—for ary

thing," she heard him say once to Mamma. "You got no idea how I hate it."

"It was Ralph Shane and your own young ones did what was done for you till the doctor came, that night," Mamma came back dryly. "So you can just forget Tom Shane. He only looked on like the rest of us."

Mamma said right out that there wouldn't be any Christmas for them this year. It wouldn't do to pester Papa when he was so upset about the cost of his accident. "I don't know whatall we're goin' to be up against," she worried. "We've not had anything like this before. Lord only knows how much those X rays will cost. I know I got to keep Papa from worryin' all I can. It's too bad about the little ones. Maybe—maybe Jenny won't even know it is Christmas if Leeroy'll keep his mouth shut."

"I'll get him to promise," Enie said miserably. But she kept putting it off, and two days before Christmas she was making up the front room bed and saw Mr. Shane's car pull up at the gate. Mr. Tom and Mrs. Shane got out, Mr. Tom carrying a large cardboard box. Enie hurried to the door, wishing she had got the bed done; she couldn't ask the Shanes back to the kitchen where Papa sat whittling by the stove.

"We can't stay," Mrs. Shane assured Enie on the heels of her hurried greeting. "We just wanted to inquire after your father. We're on our way to meet Rowan's train." Mrs. Shane's face went suddenly pink above the soft fur of her coat collar. "I was looking through some old stuff in the attic and I came across so many old toys of the children's— not doing a soul any good. Seems a pity for them to lie there and be eaten by roaches, doesn't it? I thought if the children could get any pleasure out of them . . ." She stopped for breath and Mr. Tom shoved the carton past Enie into the hall.

"Bunch of junk," he chuckled. "Kids always love junk. How's your daddy?"

"He's some better, thank you, sir," Enie said. Mr. Tom was already backing toward the edge of the porch. "Come on, Mother, come on. We don't want Rowie standing round in the cold at the depot."

"I'm coming. Good-by, dear, merry Christmas to you all. She trotted after Mr. Shane on her little high heels.

"Thank you, ma'am," Enie called. "Thank you, Mr. Shane." She heard Mamma coming along the hall from the back, but Mr. and Mrs. Shane were getting into the car. Enie pointed to the carton. "Look, Mamma, it's stuff for Leeroy and Jenny's Christmas! They can have one, after all."

Mamma's hand flew to her mouth. "Oh, my, oh, my. Now, if that's not good of them. They're real neighbors, I don't care what anybody says."

Papa was calling irately and Mamma said quickly, "Get that box outa here fore the younguns see." But Enie knew it was Papa she didn't want to see before he could be prepared. He would be furious at what he would consider Shane's charity. Enie dragged the box into the front room and pushed it under the bed.

Much later, when she got a chance, she stole in and looked at its contents. There was a doll as good as new and nearly as big as Jenny, golden hair tied back with a blue ribbon, starched white dress and lace-trimmed underwear that made Enie gasp with delight. A little black trunk, bound with brass, was filled with clothes to fit the doll. There was a leather pouch of marbles—every one a shining glassie, not a peewee in the lot—and, fitted carefully in the bottom of the box, a tiny engine with a string of cars and dismembered lengths of shiny track.

Enie squatted, looking at the toys a long time before she pushed the box back under the bed. Something nagged, picked at her mind, rose to the surface suddenly, light as a bubble—words so closely associated with Mamma's voice that she half turned her head to make sure Mamma was not behind her, saying them: God moves in mysterious ways His wonders to perform.

As the winter wore on, Papa found little chores for himself. He could split kindling sitting beside the woodbox. He would set a stick of wood on the edge of the box and come down expertly with the hatchet he had previously sharpened to deadly efficiency. The stick of wood split clean and thin, and the fragrance of fat pine mingled with the food odors. "I don't believe I ever had me so much good kindlin' wood," Mamma praised him. "It sure comes in handy. Anything I mortal hate to do is hafta stop my work an' split up a lightered knot."

He got out the little hand stone and sharpened all Mamma's knives and ranged them in their rack on the wall out of reach of small hands that might go meddling. He mended two skillets and the dishpan that had sprung a leak.

Mamma found things for Papa to do—a chair to repair; string, long hoarded, to untangle and wind on a corncob. He became expert at getting about, pulling the heavy cast with an agile swing of his big body between the borrowed crutches. As the cold lessened he left the house and hobbled to the lot and barn to odd jobs and the haranguing of Henry Jim or Enie at feeding and milking. And it was he who shot Doc when the old horse sickened and lay blowing raucously through inflamed and flaring nostrils.

"Lemme go get Mr. Jimmy Hightower, Pa," Henry Jim begged. "He's good at animal doctorin'. Him and Ralph Shane both are good at it."

Papa flushed under the eyes. "No use pesterin' Jimmy to come way over here. An' I don't need Shanes, I thank you. Doc ain't been worth his salt for two-three years."

Leeroy began to snuffle. "He don't do no harm, Papa . . ."

"He eats, don't he? Oughta been put away long time ago."

Enie shut her eyes and stopped her ears when Papa started toward the fence, and the gun's explosion seemed to take place inside her own head. Henry Jim had to get the Vance boys to help drag the carcass away, and Leeroy cried himself into such a coughing spell that Mama had to boil up another mess of creosote and molasses to dose him with.

Papa's restlessness increased as spring approached. It was now a foregone conclusion that Henry Jim would drop out of school when the time came. He didn't care, but Mamma felt bad about it. Henry Jim made the mistake of saying it would have been a good thing if Papa had bought that tractor T.H. had talked about before he went away.

"Tractor!" Papa roared, slamming a chunk of lightwood into the box so the wall trembled behind it. "All you younguns think about is buying and spending. They ain't nothing to spend, can't you get that through your heads? How much you think this leg has cost me, with them X rays just so the doc could look at these busted bones? Besides the doc's visits an' them pills to stop the pain an' all the rest of it. Be more of it, likely, when this durned plaster wall comes off'n my leg. What in tarnation would I buy a tractor with?"

"I just said it would of come in handy."

"A new leg'd come in handy, too, but I got to do with this broke-down, patched-up thing."

"Now, Clement," Mamma pleaded, "your leg's better; it'll be all right when you need it the worst. You see if it's not."

"That don't stop what it's already cost me, or what it will fore I'm done—if I ever am." The bitterness in Papa's voice filled the room and touched them all with a heavy hand.

When Dr. Helms took the cast off Papa's leg late in February, the family stood around with bated breath. The leg was dead-white with patches of rash here and there, hairless, slightly shrunken. He got up, sweating, and put his weight on it. They could see it tremble, but it did not give. He limped across the room, dragging it a little, like Ralph Shane. Dr. Helms had done a good job and Papa was a healthy man. Though he must limp for a little while, the leg would be entirely well, Dr. Helms promised him, and Papa believed it at last, though he chafed at having to be careful.

By the middle of March tractors were turning the many acres belonging to Mr. Tom Shane; Howells', Vances' and Elkins'. Mules drew plows through the others, the small, poor ones, and the *haws* and *gees* and *hummups* rang out all day across the new furrows. Henry Jim quit school, and neighbors took turns at helping a lamed man and a boy put in a crop. Enie did most of the housework out of school hours to spare Mamma, who was poorly again. Washday was changed from Monday to Saturday so she could manage the brunt of it. The topic of her valedictory address was chosen, and Mr. Agnew helped her with its preparation. By the middle of April she was memorizing and rehearsing the delivery of her speech.

14

THE EXPENSES of graduation took shape relentlessly. First there were the rings. Gold, with the year inscribed in gold upon a disk of onyx. When the picure in the salesman's catalog went round at the special class meeting, Enic thought she would almost as soon have a ring like this as the one with the emerald she intended to possess some day. But she knew Papa would think she was out of her mind—and tell her so—if she asked for eight dollars to spend on one finger just because she was about to be graduated from Green Pine High School.

Otis and Lou Addie Jason did not have the money for rings either, so Enie was spared the embarrassment of being the only member of the class who would not wear one on graduation night. There was, however, no getting out of the cap and gown rental—seventy-five cents per graduate—or the formal gown for the senior banquet at the Grandview Hotel. The Grandview was a three-story brick building at the head of Main Street, its grandest view being the railroad tracks and a scattered row of stores with corrugated iron roof extensions. This fact in no wise dimmed the glory of the banquet, and Enie, valedictorian of her class, could not very well fail to appear and it must be in an evening gown.

When, finally, she told Mamma about the required finery she got the surprise of her life. Mamma said nothing, but there was almost a twinkle in her eye as she got her old purse down from the wardrobe shelf. Enie watched her take a handful of crumpled bills from it. "See can you make that do," she said, laying them grandly in Enie's lap.

Enie stared at Mamma for a moment, then counted the money slowly. Three five-dollar bills and five ones. Twenty dollars! "Mamma! How—where—with Papa's accident and all, how did you . . ." Mamma chuckled.

"Pshaw, child. I been knowing for four years you had to have a graduation day, haven't I? I'd of gone on relief like Atkinses 'fore I'd have let this go for ary other purpose." She looked at her hands. "You'll have to order your dress. I wouldn't tackle the making of a thing like that."

Enie nearly wore out the two colored pages of Sears Roebuck devoted to formal wear, and finally settled on a blue rayon taffeta with tight-fitting bodice and full, flowing skirt with an overskirt of net. It cost twelve dollars and ninety-five cents, leaving enough money for shoes and a pair of silk stockings.

It was the day the dress arrived that Enie began to worry in earnest about Mamma. The dress was a little big in the waist and a bit too long, and Mamma took it up, getting down stiffly to pin the hem, handling her needle clumsily because of the stiffness in her finger joints. When the alterations were done, she brought out an old sheet to wrap it in against soiling and Enie hung it in the wardrobe. Turning from the balky door that always stuck, she saw Mamma clutching at her chest, a look of pain twisting her face.

"What is it, Mamma? What's the matter?"

After a long, frightening moment, Mamma said, breathlessly, "Nothin'. Just that stitch I get sometimes. It'll be gone in a minute."

It was gone in a minute, but Mamma was pale and moved cautiously for some time afterwards, and worry crept into Enie's graduation excitement, making her forget the dress for a while. She begged Mamma to go to the doctor on Saturday but Mamma brushed the plea aside with a laugh. "Everybody has to slow down when they get to my age—specially after a hard winter like we just been through. I'll make me up a mess of tonic tomorrow."

Everything seemed to Enie to move at a frightening pace now. It seemed strange to think she had ever chafed at the dragging of time. Before she could believe it, the night of the banquet had come and she was sitting next to Otis Jason at the long table in the dining room of the Grandview Hotel. She was impressed by the snowy cloth, the generous and somewhat bewildering array of silver at each place, the enormous centerpeice of gladioli flanked by tall twisted tapers weeping blobs of wax down their sides. There was ice cream—wonderfully made in the class colors—an after-dinner speech by a red-faced class president, a final singsong with Mary Lee Williams at the piano. Mr. Agnew sat beside her—to turn the music, he said, though most of the songs were sung—and played—from memory.

All the last week of school—a week crowded with commencement activities—Enie's speech was always at the back of her mind, and more than once she started from her night's sleep, mumbling the words she had rehearsed so many times. Twice that week she heard Mamma getting up in the night for baking soda. Sometimes Enie had a crazy feeling that she wouldn't make it, after all; that she would never receive the diploma. She tried to push the threat away, but it persisted, sly and shadowy, formless yet always there.

On Friday before commencement Mr. Orin Thompson left a parcel in the mailbox for Enie. She stared at the name written in Miss Pritchard's handwriting. When her butterfingers got the string and wrappings off, there was a beautiful loose-leaf notebook bound in real leather, with *Earline Singleton* lettered in gold upon the back.

Enie laid the book in Mamma's lap, unable to speak as Mamma examined it with proper reverence. "You see? I knowed she'd not forget you. You meant as much to her as she did to you, Enie."

The next day—Saturday—Mamma took to her bed and did not get up again. "If I can get me some sleep, I'll be better. I can't run the risk of not being fit to see you march in with the rest tomorrow at the sermon."

With a heavy heart Enie sent the children to play by the branch and hurried through the housework so as to have time to wash her hair before starting dinner. If I can just get graduated, she thought desperately, if I can just get through, I'll spend the whole enduring summer taking care of Mamma. Whether I read a line or write a word. I won't mention college or hate Papa any more. If I can just graduate Monday night. I'll be glad and grateful to spend the summer nursing Mamma. I'll make her well . . . It was a prayer going through her head all morning.

When Mamma didn't touch her dinner, Enie begged to be allowed to get the doctor. "It won't take me any time to run down to Vances' and phone." But Mamma insisted that all she needed was to lie quiet. "Don't take on so, Enie, I'll be all right."

Enie's gown flowed over the ironing board like a

great, dark tent, the edges touching the floor. When it was pressed she hung it on a peg behind the door in her room, the cap perched rakishly above it. She touched the silken tassel and a thrill went through her. The day of days was near, indeed; what *could* stop it now except the end of the world?

She went down to the branch to go through her speech once more, vowing it was for the last time. standing on the rock, her hands clasped tensely in front of her—"loosely, Earline, relax; don't stand like a wooden Indian"—Mr. Agnew's voice seemed to echo in the willows. She went through the address from beginning to end without a bobble. Superimposed upon her consciousness were the sounds of Jenny's and Leeroy's playing, and once, they stole near, peering at her, giggling behind muddy hands. She motioned them away without interrupting the flow of her speech.

When Papa and Henry Jim came home from town, Leeroy and Jenny shone from yellow soap and pump water, and Mamma was still asleep. "I'll have me a good all-over bath after supper," Enie promised herself, feeling in imagination the cool water on her limbs and sticky body. She would lie, clean, in her thin nightgown and think about tomorrow. The baccalaureate address would be delivered by a visiting minister in the high school auditorium, and Earline Singleton would march at the head of the line with Mary Lee Williams behind her. She would occupy the first seat in the first of the two reserved front rows. She would be wearing her cap and gown, scholarly, dignified. It should be a good thought to fall asleep on.

After the others had eaten, Enie sent Leeroy to see if Mamma had awakened. He came back, round-eyed. "She called me T. H.," he said, twisting his overall button. "Might be she couldn't see me good, it's kinda dark in there."

Enie and Henry Jim exchanged startled glances; Papa got up from the table and limped to the front room. Enie was removing the dishes when he said from the door, "I better go see can I get aholt of Doc Helms."

Enie began to wash the dishes, paying no attention to Leeroy's questions. Henry Jim did a thing completely out of character. He got a towel and started drying the dishes Enie took from the pan. Suddenly he broke out furiously, "Some folks have all the luck, and some don't have a durn bit!"

Enie sent Leeroy to bed and helped Jenny with her buttons. Papa came back and went at once to the front room; Enie was afraid to go in. She crept out to the dark porch, and Henry Jim followed her like an uneasy shadow. They sat and stared toward the road; when a pair of headlights fanned brightness along it, Henry Jim said huskily, "That must be him."

Dr. Helms stayed a long time, and when he came out Papa was with him. They paid no attention to Enie and Henry Jim crouched on the edge of the porch. "You understand, Clem, absolute quiet. Another attack—and she could go like that." He cracked his fingers. "I'll be back in the morning. That hypo will get her through the night all right. But she's got to have quiet and care for a long time."

———

So Mamma did not see Enie march in to the slow magnificence of the processional.

Miss Sadie Hightower came and stayed so Papa could go with the children to the commencement sermon. He sat, solemn and churchly, in his good suit along with the other families of the graduates, Henry Jim, Leeroy and Jenny strung out beside him. The whole program was like a bad dream to Enie—a dream from which she must wake and worry about her speech perhaps; just now her mind was almost comfortably encased in the shock of Dr. Helms's words last night.

All commencement Sunday Mamma rested peacefully, sleeping, half-rousing to sleep again. Everybody knew of her illness now, and a wordless tide of sympathy flowed toward Enie who was too numb to receive it. Before daylight the pain came again, worse than it had ever been. Henry Jim raced the pickup to Vances' to call Dr. Helms; he came and gave Mamma a hypodermic of morphine. He said only that she would sleep, but his face, grim and sad in the yellow lamplight, told

Enie the truth. It sank into her mind, terrible and unalterable.

On his way out, Dr. Helms put his hand on Enie's arm. "You're going to graduate tonight, aren't you, Sis?" Enie nodded. "That's fine. I hear there's a big class this year. Like to hear that. Like for young folks to learn. Wish we could ever learn half enough." Anger spurted in his eyes, died as quickly as it had come. "Sade's coming back to spend the night. She'll bring her cot she takes on confinements and be right with your mother. Everything will be all right." But Enie noticed he turned his look from her.

Darkness came, bringing Enie's great night, the culmination of years of dreams—a nightmare, after all. Once more the heavy, solemn strains of the *Pomp and Circumstance* march pounded through the little auditorium, the high school band making only a few mistakes; the audience rose respectfully, necks craning eagerly. The graduates marched in, sweating and pale with the heat of the dark gowns and their own dreadful concentration. The school board members were ranged impressively on the stage; each graduate's chair awaited its occupant. The night had come. None of them quite believed it, Enie least of all. Down front, watching her, were all the members of her family except T.H. and Mamma.

Mary Lee Williams delivered her salutatorian's address and Enie heard it mechanically; she knew every word of it as well as she knew her own speech. Her hands did not pluck at the folds of her gown but lay quietly in her lap, as they never had at rehearsals. She was a vast, weightless vacuum of waiting. Her turn was next. She heard the applause for Mary Lee, saw her walk to her chair, the tassel of her cap swinging as she sat down, the dimple in her flushed cheek.

Enie heard her own voice without remembering that she had walked to the front of the stage; it was clear and unshaken, the voice of a stranger. She did not think at all, only spoke, exactly as she had been taught to do, to the end. Applause burst from the audience. Mr. Claye, the principal, turned and broke his mask of dignity to smile at her. Tears came to her eyes and she sat, straight and stiff, seeing rainbows round the footlights. All she had to do now was walk up and receive her diploma when her name was called.

Mary Lee Williams was giving a party for all the seniors after the exercises. She came hesitantly across to Enie in the classroom where the caps and gowns were to be left. "Can't you come, Enie? It might make you feel better." The kindness in Mary Lee's voice was a thing to remember after all the strife between them. Enie folded her gown carefully and laid it on the pile on the teacher's desk. "I can't, Mary Lee, thank you kindly. Papa's waiting for me."

Mary Lee lingered awkwardly. "You said your speech real well," she said. Enie looked at her. "You did, too." They smiled. It was as if, in that moment, they both grew up, and everything mean and ugly and childish was forever washed away.

Jenny fell asleep in Enie's arms as the truck bumped along the road. Miz Sade came out to greet them with the statement that Mamma hadn't so much as turned over while they were gone. The good rest might do wonders for her. "Roscoe brought over some co'cola and a sorry old cake I stirred up this morning. Come eat some, if you can get it down."

They sat round the table in the kitchen, drinking the ice-cold Coca-Cola and eating the "sorry old cake" that melted in their mouths with goodness. Miz Sade unrolled Enie's diploma and said solemnly, "That is a thing to be mighty proud of, honey. It's going to pleasure your mamma a sight."

"Take it in there, Miz Sade," Enie said, looking at her hands. "She might wake up in the night."

Jenny began to cry and beg for Mamma, so Enie took her into bed with her. When she had quieted the child, Enie fell into a heavy, heartless sleep of exhaustion. When she woke the sun was shining in the window and Jenny was playing at the foot of her bed. Enie lay, sensing a difference in the day; she had graduated from high school last night, of course, but there was something else. Suddenly she knew, and it was more remarkable than her graduation: Papa had not banged on the wall. She got up at once and hurried into her clothes.

Miz Sade did not leave Mamma, and Papa and Henry Jim did not go to the field that day. Once, Henry Jim said to Enie, "Willy Vance and Ralph Shane are hoeing the beans." Enie did not answer. Eventually it was dusk and Dr. Helms was there. Papa stood in the kitchen door chewing his lip. He jerked his head toward Enie. "She wants to see you."

In the gaunt transparency of her face Mamma's eyes had a luminous beauty. She put her hand out and Enie dropped to her knees beside the bed, forgetting Papa, Miz Sade, and the doctor standing about the door.

"Papa said you done good, Enie, at the exercises. I'm so proud." Enie's fingers felt along Mamma's knotted knuckles. "I knowed you would. My little girl youngun the head of that big class in the town school! You don't want to forget that."

"I won't, Mamma."

"You finished high school like I wanted you to. And Leeroy and Jenny—they will, too; I know you'll see to it. I put my dependence in you, Enie. You'll take good care of them."

"I will, Mamma, but . . ." It was hard to see Mamma's face for tears, but she clung tightly to the cold hand. Mamma's other hand fumbled over the quilt till her fingers closed gently about the roll of sheepskin beside her. She smiled.

"T.H.—" Mamma faltered, "he never . . . got here, did he?" The fingers about Enie's diploma went slack and it rolled from their weak grasp a little way across the quilt.

"I'm here, Mamma *I'm* here with you." Her voice was too loud in the quiet room. She heard Papa whisper urgently, "The others. Hadn't we ought to call them?" Someone answered, "Sh . . . In a minute . . ."

Enie pressed her body against the side of the bed. She saw Mamma's eyes half close, saw a tear's sudden gleam in the hollow of her cheek. Mamma's head drooped to one side. Enie looked up and saw Papa's fingers spread across his face. Dr. Helms stepped forward and gently drew Enie to her feet.

15

E^NIE SPENT^ all her time sitting still and staring at nothing. Not crying or brooding. Not even thinking—all of her a queer, light emptiness. Until Aunt Pearl came to her, slipped her skinny little tough arms about Enie's shoulders and asked her to help put Mamma's things away.

Enie wept then. When they brushed and aired and hung the few dresses in the wardrobe. When she straightened the fold in a dress, when she climbed on a chair to push Mamma's hat, wrapped in newspaper, back on the shelf. Aunt Pearl cried nearly all the time—cried and talked, interspersing her talk with frantic searchings about her person for the handkerchief she couldn't keep track of.

"Poor Elnora. She never did make the best of herself. Reckon she felt like it wasn't no use." She touched Mamma's apron to her red-rimmed eyes.

"Don't you be like that, Enie, you make the most of what you've got. Don't bury your talents in a napkin like it says in the Book."

"Mamma never did that, Aunt Pearl."

"No, I don't reckon she did. But she never was one to ask anything for herself, neither. What I say is, you got to ask—or take!—or get left out."

In a week, Uncle Jud came for Aunt Pearl, and she was crying when they drove away, the rouge on her thin cheeks standing out bright and crude. Enie thought it might get better now—better still when the neighbor women forgot her and left her to grapple with life as she must live it. It was hers, such as it was, and she must find a way to bear it, to take hold and do more than just make out. She had given her word to take care of Leeroy and Jenny; it wouldn't do to think beyond that just now.

As the days slipped into weeks, Mamma's friends did come less often to advise, kept at home with their own families and the tasks they were never without. The heat increased, the crop flourished, the clay mound of Mamma's grave dried, with the wreaths upon it like the ones on little Sue Ann's. The Singletons were a small family now, without Mamma, T.H. and Sue Ann.

It never occurred to Enie to go to Papa for help, that the common grief might draw them together, wipe out old hurts and angers; the old wall stood high as ever between them, and Enie struggled alone with the problems Mamma had left her.

There was the trouble with Leeroy. Lost and bewildered in the grief he could not understand, he rebelled at Enie's new authority, screaming that she was not the boss of him and to shut her big mouth. Enie's remorse at the slaps and scoldings she administered only added misery to her heavy heart. Then one morning after breakfast Papa said, "Git your hat, Leeroy. You got to help me and Henry Jim with them snap beans. They're comin' on faster than I allowed they would."

Enie turned round from the stove, saying the first thing that came into her head. "I counted on Leeroy to help me at the house, Papa."

"He goin' to do gal work all his life? Leeroy's going on ten year old. T.H. and Henry Jim was startin' to plow when they were twelve."

"They were hardier than Leeroy. Mamma had me to help in the house; I need somebody. Jenny's not big enough."

"What's to do here?" Papa's eyes went impatiently round the cluttered kitchen. "Woman work that don't take no time to do."

"I was aiming to put up some tomatoes, so I wouldn't get in a rush with all the canning at once. It takes a heap of stovewood ..."

"Box is full and piled up." Papa pointed out inexorably. "I don't begrudge you the help you need, girl. But my need's consid'able you got to admit." He jerked his hat from the nail, his eyes hard on Leeroy.

Enie dropped pretense. "Leeroy's just naturally

not hardy enough for field work, Papa. He'll be down with the summer complaint if he stays out in the hot sun. Mamma would never let him—if she was here."

The silence in the kitchen swelled, a dusky flush came up in Papa's face. He pulled his hat over his eyes and limped out of the kitchen.

Enie sat down and put her hands over her face. In spite of her lifelong fear of Papa she had stood up to him and beaten him. After a moment she felt a timid touch on the back of her neck. Leeroy stood beside her. "Don't cry, Enie," he whispered. "You feel bad about Mamma?" Enie nodded, looking at Leeroy through her tears.

"Me, too. I feel awful bad—worsen when I've got my cough, right here." He touched his chest. "I wisht she was here like she uster be." It was the first reference he had made to Mamma's going. Enie lifted the edge of her skirt and wiped her eyes.

"Wishing won't do any good, Leeroy. But if you'd try to be good and mind me—I have to take Mamma's place the best I know how—it would make her happy."

Leeroy ran a dirty finger along the back of Enie's chair. "You reckon she can see me?"

"Maybe. I don't know."

"Well, *I* don't reckon she can," Leeroy said flatly. "Not in that hole in the ground where they put her."

"Mamma's not in the ground," Enie denied passionately. "It's just the sick, used-up part of her that she doesn't need any more that's there. There's something else—the spirit of her that can't be lost."

"Where at, heaven?"

"Well, I guess so—at least, they call it that."

Leeroy tucked his underlip beneath the two big front teeth that pointed out like a squirrel's. He said nothing but his eyes were unbelieving, telling Enie he had seen them put Mamma in the ground.

That night after Papa had gone to bed, Henry Jim said to Enie, "You gonna make a sissy outa that kid if you don't watch out."

"I don't care," Enie retorted. "I know what Mamma would do. And so do you."

Next day when she had finished the housework, Enie herself went to the field. Mamma would not have approved of that either, but it was the only compromise she could settle upon to insure the permanence of her victory for Leeroy. She left him in charge of Jenny and he crossed his heart and hoped to die if he meddled with the fire or went beyond the lot fence.

She was a fast worker and her quick hands made a marked difference, but Papa had a deadline to meet for Mr. Beazely of the canning factory, and the three pickers worked with backbreaking steadiness. On what Papa said must be the last day of the picking, Ralph Shane rode to the edge of the field on Sweet Lou. He limped to Papa's row and said casually, "Looks like you've raised more of a crop than you've got hands to harvest, Mr. Clem. I can take a few turns with you if you don't mind."

Papa shook the sweat out of his eyes and grunted something that was not rejection, yet scarcely acceptance either. Enie, squatting on her filthy sneakers, saw Ralph Shane hunker down and begin to pick. She knew Papa did not want the help of a Shane, that he resented it as patronage amounting to insult, but he could not prevent it without breaking the oldest law he knew: in times of stress one man helped another. He would have to accept and give Ralph Shane "much obliged" at least, no matter how he felt about it. She bent her hot face over the bucket she had half filled in the last fifteen minutes.

The afternoon hours slid by. Sweet Lou stood patiently at the edge of the field, switching flies, cropping clumps of green, and Ralph Shane picked beans as though his living depended upon it. There was no talk among them; and when Papa's bushel basket was full, it was Ralph who reached for another. Papa scarcely looked up, only pushed his hat back to scratch his head and moved on thick haunches down the row, away from Ralph.

Enie lifted her full pail and walked down the row to empty it into the basket. She stood so near Ralph she could see the sweat straining the back of his shirt, feel the heat radiating from his body. He was bareheaded in the brutal sun, his hair glinting against the red-brown of his strong neck. Enie's eyes roved from Ralph's neck to the ragged brim of Papa's hat, his soaked blue shirt she would wash on Monday, his thick crimson neck. Why was Ralph Shane working alongside Papa like a hired field hand? He had worked on Papa's land when Mamma died—but everything was different at a time like that; surely it could only be that now he wished to show friendship and neighborliness. If Papa would only take it as it was offered, as any other farmer's help. But she was certain he wouldn't; it would be like the toys the Christmas he was hurt—the kind deed twisted by suspicion and resentment. She almost wished Ralph hadn't come to help them.

The sun was still high and hot when Enie dumped her last bucketful into Henry Jim's basket. Her head throbbed with weariness and her dress stuck to her body. She looked at Papa; he would have to thank Ralph now, no matter what he thought. But it was Henry Jim who spoke up. "We're sure obliged to you, Ralph. We'd not of got done if you hadn't pitched in like you did."

Ralph laughed. "Oh, you would, I guess. But I had the time; don't know any better way to use it."

"Might be we could help you out—sometime," Henry Jim said awkwardly.

"Might be," Ralph agreed. "Just glad I happened along."

Papa frowned at the baskets heaped with beans.

Drops of sweat hung like jewels from his eyebrows. He shifted his game leg and little puffs of dust came up round his shoes. "I'm much obliged to you," he said, the words coming, shamed, from the depths of his stubborn pride. He chewed his lip. "You're a fast picker, I'll say that."

Enie found her own silence unendurable, suddenly; she was not only grateful to Ralph for his help, she felt a sort of triumph in the proof he had given Papa and Henry Jim that Tom Shane's bookish, crippled boy could work as well as the next man. She said quickly, over a painful shyness, "We'd be proud to have you take supper with us, such as it is."

Ralph put his hand on her shoulder right before Papa and Henry Jim. "Not tonight, Enie, thanks just the same. Rowie's got company up at the house and I'm expected to be there."

Enie and Henry Jim watched as he mounted Sweet Lou and started down the road, but Papa lifted a basket to his shoulder and headed for the house.

"That mare must be getting kind of old," Henry Jim said. "Seems like he's been ridin' her ever since I can recollect." He gave Enie a sly glance. "You sweet on him?"

"No, I'm not sweet on him," Enie retorted, but she felt the blush going down into her neck. "You take hold of this other handle. I got to get to the house. Those younguns have been left by themselves long enough."

That night, after the others had gone to bed, Enie brought out Mamma's calico quilt and lay on the porch, looking up at the stars. They always made her remember Seedy Culpepper. Nowhere, Seedy had told them, were stars so big and bright and close as in Alabama on a summer night. They did look enormous, low-swung and bright beyond the edge of the roof. Watching them made Enie feel a little lightheaded. From star-gazing it seemed hardly a step to thoughts of Ralph Shane. She wondered why he never went courting girls; was it because of being lame—he was only a little lame, maybe because of Bliss Atkins? But that was so long ago, and Bliss was no longer in Tired Creek. Her heart quickened a little. Maybe he'd never found a girl to suit him . . .

A star went streaking down the sky like a rocket. That, as every boy and girl knew, was a sign given by the heavens for a kiss. If Ralph were here with her now, would he kiss her? The screen door creaked open and Papa's bulk, shapeless in his nightshirt, filled the doorway. He stepped forward, letting the door slap softly to behind him. "You aimin' to spend the night out here?"

"It's so hot in the house," Enie complained, pulling her skirt over her legs.

"Hit is close," Papa agreed. Enie watched him cross the porch and ease himself to the floor with a grunt. "Hard on a workin' man not to git his rest." He tipped his face to the sky. "Nary a sign of rain. Could be a bad drought workin' up. I recollect seven years ago we had one burnt ever last livin' thing to a pure crisp. Didn't hardly git table vittles out of all the crops put in."

Enie felt uneasy at Papa's sociability and said nothing as she watched him warily. He leaned his head against the post and sighed. Enie had the feeling that there was something on his mind he could not get around to coming out with. "Heat lightnin'," he scoffed, as a pallid glow quivered against the horizon. "Don't mean nothin'. Your ma used to say hit was pretty. She thought a heap of things was pretty—sun risin' an' settin', moon, stars, heat lightnin'."

Enie moved her palms along her face, over the sharp ridges of her cheekbones, rested them against her eyelids. If he didn't stop talking about Mamma she would be blubbering like a baby. He said then, abruptly, "What in tarnation made young Shane pick them beans? Been anybody else I wouldn't of thought nothing about it, but how come him to?"

Enie sighed. "I reckon he just wanted to be neighborlike, Papa. He's a farmer's son—even if he does read books. He knows how it is when folks are hard-pressed . . ."

"Him?" Papa shifted his weight and the post creaked. "Shanes don't have no hard times. There's my piece of land Tom Shane's been after and ain't never going to get."

"Papa," Enie protested, "that's not the reason Ralph helped us, I know it's not. Maybe Mr. Tom is greedy, but that doesn't make Ralph so!" She felt Papa's eyes boring into her.

"He's a Shane, ain't he? And them Shanes want the earth. Want to be ahead of everybody else. Got to have the most and the best. Got to have the whole durn world fore they're done, or tear up the patch tryin' to get it." He stood up. "I said I was obliged for the help. Only thing is . . ." He hesitated so long that Enie stirred uneasily. "Only thing is, it better be my land he had on his mind, not nothing else."

"What do you mean, Papa?" Enie asked. Papa picked his steps carefully round her pallet, moved toward the door.

"I mean that I got a girl that's motherless. I aim to make mighty sure there's no carryin' on to cause talk." The door closed behind him and Enie lay flat and still, too stunned for anger.

Slowly the numbness passed and longing for her mother possessed her, bearing down like a physical pain. A tiny breeze wandered across her motionless body, and inside the house Leeroy cried out sharply from the torment of a nightmare. Enie dragged herself up, gathered the quilt in her arms, and went in to quiet him.

16

THE DROUGHT Papa feared did not come. Work reached its crest and lessened, and it was time for the revival. Papa did not speak of attending till Miss Elsie Mae Howells came to the house and urged him to go.

She came on a Sunday afternoon, driving her brother's Ford car and wearing a big chip straw hat with a cascade of lavender flowers on the side of it. She had never been at the Singleton's before except for Sue Ann's and Mamma's funerals, and her flamboyant cheer seemed to overflow the place. Enie held Jenny on her lap throughout the visit and covertly wished Miss Elsie Mae would go.

She had heard Miss Elsie Mae was in her forties, but she didn't look that old. Her ways were not those of other Tired Creek women; she was a little loud and silly, Enie thought. She knew Miss

Elsie Mae had seen a younger sister married off and leaving her single, and that after her parents' death she had kept house for her brother Sonny, and dedicated herself to church music on the side.

"Come here, sugar," Miss Elsie Mae coaxed Jenny. "Come sit on my lap." But Jenny leaned hard against Enie and sucked her finger. Miss Elsie Mae opened her big white purse and took out some picture cards. "Want these—to keep?" she tempted, and Jenny slid out of Enie's lap, finally, and crossed the porch to Miss Elsie Mae Howells.

Miss Elsie Mae had a great deal to say to Papa about how the meeting was progressing, but loudly deplored his absence. "That choir just isn't a choir without your bass, Mr. Singleton, I declare. We can't get along without it and I told them so." She giggled—more like a high school girl than a settled woman. "They appointed me a committee of one to call on you and ask if you couldn't make it to the evening services." She twisted a lock of Jenny's hair about her finger. "They don't commence till seven-thirty." She dropped her eyes modestly. "Of course, we all understand how you feel about mingling with folks just now—but it would be a real blessing if you would come and sing for the Lord."

The upshot of it was that Papa promised to go. At first Enie was glad, for it brought a change in him. He liked to sing in the choir, and he and Miss

Elsie Mae Howells would discuss the music at length after the service, while Enie waited in the pickup, Leeroy whining and Jenny asleep and the mosquitoes biting them and Henry Jim showing off before a cluster of giggling girls.

After the revival ended with baptizing in the creek, school started; then fall came—whispering of better things to Enie. Of less work and more energy for what there was, of—perhaps—a time for writing and reading, if she could get over to Shanes' without Papa knowing, to borrow a few books. In the woods persimmons turned and slowly ripened till, after the first hard frost, they would be sweet enough to eat. Chestnuts fell in the grove behind Elkins'; pecans burst from their outer hulls and dropped like big slow drops of rain among their crisping leaves, others clinging stubbornly to be flailed from their branches by Leeroy and other little boys who climbed nimbly among the trees and thrashed the nuts down with long poles. Leeroy worked, Saturdays, in Mr. Tom Shane's groves, earning an impressive pile of quarters to go into the tobacco tin that held his savings for the bicycle he meant to buy.

The light changed subtly, the color of the sky night and morning, and even the hot noontime held a new vastness in its scope, calling once more to Enie's mind the bigness of a world outside Tired Creek.

But Miss Elsie Mae Howells' interest in the Singleton family had not stopped with the revival. As summer faded into autumn and autumn succumbed to winter, it increased. For a time she claimed that she came to talk to Papa about the church music, but Enie knew it was only a pretext. She knew Miss Elsie Mae was after Papa; he was a widower and Miss Elsie Mae was a man-crazy old maid. Her visits were marked by offerings—cake, still warm from the oven, gew-gaws from the dime store for Leeroy and Jenny.

Enie's sense of outrage mounted with each trivial gift, each kindness to herself and the children. They were all, for Enie, lures to ensnare Papa. And Mamma lying in her grave only a few months. Enie came to loathe the smell of Miss Elsie Mae's lavishly applied perfume, the sound of her nervous giggle, the flash of her youthful clothes.

On an evening late in September Miss Elsie Mae was with them on the porch. The air was fresh with autumn coolness and a moon was rising, nearly full, over the cane patch across the road. Miss Elsie Mae had possessed herself of Mamma's rocker and every squeak of it echoed angrily in Enie's mind. Miss Elsie Mae had brought chewing gum this time as well as the hymnal with certain songs marked to show Papa—as if he didn't know every hymn in the book backward and forward—

and they were all chewing like a bunch of cows at their cuds.

Papa had been gruff tonight, downright unsociable in fact, moving his chair out in the yard and tipping it back against the chinaberry tree. Enie could see it hadn't fazed Miss Elsie Mae any more than her own unyielding coldness.

"I got to be going," she said, and didn't stir. "Play us a piece on your harp, Leeroy."

Leeroy, sitting beside Enie on the step, blew gently into the harmonica, and after a few aimless strains it began to sound like music. He kept it soft, but there was a wildness somewhere underneath the softness that seemed to come from the secret depths of Leeroy.

"I declare he's got talent," Miss Elsie Mae said. "It ought not to be wasted on a little old harp." She rocked a moment. "I could teach that boy to play the piano if his daddy was willing. He could come up to my house. It's kind of slack time for me right now; I haven't got but two pupils and I'd be glad to give Leeroy lessons free. It'd be pure pleasure to work with a little feller with so much music in him."

Enie said, "We haven't got a piano for him to practice on."

"He could practice at my house. I'll ask your daddy. How'd you like that, Leeroy?" Miss Elsie Mae's voice was all soft with smiles.

Enie's helplessness made her feel faint. It was not for Papa that she feared and hated these little traps; he could look out for himself or take what was coming to him. But Mamma's memory was a precious thing, jealously guarded in Enie's grieving heart—a thing she felt obliged to nurture in the little children's hearts. Had not Mamma committed them to her keeping? Almost the last words she spoke had so committed them. Enie had no intention of moving quietly aside for a schemer like Miss Elsie Mae, however kindly her intentions seemed, to usurp the love and loyalty that belonged to Mamma.

"I'd ruther play my harp than the pianer," Leeroy blurted, digging his toe in the sand.

Miss Elsie Mae was undaunted. "You'd like the piano when you got used to it," she promised, as if it were all settled. "I reckon your folks would be real proud if you turned out to be a real musician."

Enie nearly laughed out loud. She could imagine Papa's reaction to a piano-playing son. "You'd be wasting your time, Miss Elsie Mae, if you ask Papa such a thing. He'd never in this world let one of his boys take music lessons."

"Nothing ventured, nothing gained," Miss Elsie Mae said brightly. "It couldn't hurt to try, could it?"

Enie saw Papa coming across the yard, carrying his chair. He set it on the porch and looked back over his shoulder at the sky. Enie held her breath, wondering if Miss Elsie Mae would ask him now, hoping she would and receive the edge of his tongue for her pains. But Miss Elsie Mae was silent, holding Jenny in her arms as if she belonged to her already.

Leeroy began another wandering tune and Papa said, "You better git to bed, son." When Leeroy did not move, playing as if he had not heard, Papa added, "You hear me, boy? Git! Hurry up about it."

"This little nubbin's fast asleep," Miss Elsie Mae said tenderly, handing Jenny to Papa. He took Jenny in and they could hear him bumping about in the dark.

Enie sat still, heavy with sadness and a dull anger tinged with shadowy guilt; she felt that she had somehow been a party to cheating Leeroy of something.

"I got to be going," Miss Elsie Mae said once more, and this time she stood up and moved slowly toward the steps. Papa came out of the house and walked, a step or two behind her, to the car. They stood a moment, talking, and Enie could not catch a word. When Miss Elsie Mae turned on the headlights Enie went in, slamming the screen door hard after her.

It confused Enie that, while there was this with Miss Elsie Mae Howells, Papa took all the family to Pleasant Grove every Sunday to weed and tidy the plot in the graveyard, to leave such flowers as they could lay their hands on upon the two graves. His face, Enie noticed, was sad when he stood for a moment beside the larger mound, and once when Henry Jim had failed to bring the rake, Papa squatted down and drew the leaves and twigs from about the grave with his hands, moving them as carefully as if he were setting out precious new plants.

If that woman would just leave him alone everything would be all right, Enie thought then, turning away to put a stiff little bunch of zinnias on Sue Ann's grave. We can run our lives without her. I'm no kid. And I'll keep my promise to Mamma to see to Leeroy and Jenny, no matter what happens.

By the time the fields were brown with November and it was too cold to sit on the porch after dark, Miss Elsie Mae's visits had stopped; Papa was calling on her instead. On Saturday nights he washed and sleeked his hair down and put on his Sunday suit and stalked out without saying a word to any of them; there was no need; Enie knew where he was going and what he was going for. It was then that she began to talk about Mamma to Jenny.

"You recollect Mamma, don't you, Jenny?"

"Uhuh. Can I have a piece of gingerbread—"

Enie cut a piece from the spicy square and held it toward Jenny on the point of the knife. "It's not half as good as Mamma's gingerbread. I can't get it as fat and light, someway."

"It's better'n anything," Jenny declared with a full mouth, " 'cept Miss Elsie Mae's cake. I love cokenut cake best, don't you?"

"Mamma's lemon-cheese cake was better."

"I don't reckerlect lemon-cheese cake."

"Well, we just had it when there was company—all-day singings or the preacher to dinner. You can't have cake every day.

"Howellses does."

"They do not, Jenny Singleton. Nobody does—only Shanes, maybe. It's not any of our business what other folks have to eat. We've got plenty." She cut herself a piece of gingerbread, handling the knife viciously. "Look, Jenny, you recollect how Mamma looked, don't you?"

Jenny looked vague, her tongue crept out to ensnare a crumb in the corner of her mouth. "Gimme another piece, Enie, a little bitty one?"

On a sunny afternoon of that same week when Jenny was asleep, Enie was in the front room trying to write. The sheet of ruled paper bore a single sentence, and Enie had just drawn a heavy line through it when she heard a car drive up and stop at the gate. Peeking out the window, she saw Miss Elsie Mae Howells crossing the yard, her hands carefully bearing a waxed-paper-covered burden. Enie crouched low, her head below the window sill. She heard Miss Elsie Mae calling, then come into the house and walk down the hall and open the kitchen door. After a moment she came back through the house, got in her brother's car and drove away.

Enie went to the kitchen and saw the cake on the table. It was huge, covered with waxed paper through which the fresh coconut was fuzzily visible. A terrible feeling boiled up in Enie; she had to struggle with it a moment before she could walk across the room and put her hands on the china plate that bore the cake. A fly had found its way under the paper and was wiggling its busy feet ecstatically on the frosting. Enie seized the cake, rushed out to the pigpen and dumped it into the trough. Her hands shook so she could hardly hold onto the flowered plate with bits of coconut frosting adhering to its fluted edges.

Enie washed the plate and slid it under the dish towels in the safe drawer. Leeroy came from school and Jenny woke, and Enie gave them cold biscuits and blackberry jam that had scorched a little in the making, last summer, due to her inexperience.

She chose an afternoon a week later to return the plate, which she had wrapped heavily in newspaper. She did not answer when Leeroy asked what she had in her hand.

"You and Jenny stay right here in the yard. If you get cold you can go in the house, but don't mess with the fire. I'm going down the road a piece, I won't be long. If you do like I tell you, I'll give you something when I get back."

"Money?" Leeroy asked hopefully.

"No. But I'll find you something—something I've been saving for when you're extra good."

The November wind was sharp with promised cold. It whipped the ends of Enie's hair out behind her and she hunched her thin shoulders, walking as fast as she could, seeing the dead leaves swirl at the road's edge. She passed the big oak where Seedy Culpepper had first kissed her, feeling only that it was a time long gone by, the kiss and the thrill of it dead as the cornstalks in the field.

The Vance and Elkins houses were behind her and she could see Shanes' chimneys above the distant trees when she turned in at the lane leading to Howells'. The house was broad and low, painted brown with green window blinds. The front yard was sandy and clean-swept, the walk leading to the steps lined with bricks. A wide porch aproned the front of the house and extended round one side where a door opened into the dining room. Enie had partaken of a wedding feast in that room when Miss Elsie Mae's younger sister married one of the Hightower boys.

She was a little girl then, but the scene had been important enough to retain a sharp clarity over the years. She recalled exactly the oval table laden with food, the bright-grained golden oak chairs, the sideboard with a mirror in a curlycue frame, the glass-sided china cabinet. She was sure it was all still there, waiting for Miss Elsie Mae and Papa to stand at the head of the table and cut the wedding cake. She knew just how the strong, white, piano-playing hands would wield the cake knife; she could hear the nervous, high giggle.

Enie twisted the old-fashioned bell handle, hoping Miss Elsie Mae would be out gadding and she could leave the plate between the screen door and the wooden one with its splendid oval of plate glass set in the middle. But she heard steps; the door opened and Miss Elsie Mae stood there, her face lighting with pleasure.

"Why, Enie Singleton! Come right in. I declare I'm proud to see you. I about decided you was never going to come to see me."

"I just came to bring back your plate, Miss Elsie Mae," Enie said. "I can't come in. It's getting late and the kids are by themselves. I thank you kindly— for the cake. You ought not to take so much trouble on yourself about us. We're doing all right." She looked Miss Elsie Mae in the eye, knowing her hint would not take, knowing too— and for the first time—that nothing is so hard to fight as kindness.

"Well, you can come in a minute anyhow, child. That's too long a walk to start right back without anything to eat or resting a minute. I'd run you back, but Son took the car. You come right on in, now."

"No ma'am, I can't, not even a minute. I just wanted to say much obliged and say the cake was—was mighty good." She bit her lip, remembering the lusty squeals of the pigs that day over the unexpected treat.

"Oh, pshaw, Enie, I wish you wouldn't be in such a hurry. Why didn't you bring the children? I could have made 'em some syrup candy to pull."

"Oh, they get enough to eat, I reckon." She

knew her rudeness had hurt Miss Elsie Mae, but she didn't care. She turned and was running down the walk, hearing Miss Elsie Mae calling but not turning, seeing the remembered dining room; the fine parlor, too, with the silk-shaded lamp on the center table, the plush sofa and platform rocker, the piano against the darkly flowered wallpaper. Leeroy said there was a radio, now, too . . .

She ran down the little lane and into the road where, gradually, she slowed to a walk, her hand pressed to the stitch in her side. The shadows stretched longer, the wind seemed to be dying tonight, she thought. She walked the last quarter of a mile with her hands tucked into her armpits, as the winter dusk dropped swiftly.

17

___

Now that the winter had come, Enie found time to write, but it availed her little. She was always worrying her problem as a dog worries a bone, and it would not recede even when she sat down with her pencil and paper. When the wind rattled the panes and banged the shutters she moped about like an unhappy ghost, shutting her ears to the children's play, feeling that she must *do* something about Papa but not knowing how to go about it. If I just had somebody to talk to about it, she thought, somebody like Miss Pritchard . . .

Enie and Henry Jim were alone in the kitchen the next time Papa walked out of the house in his good suit. Enie could contain herself no longer. "They make me sick!" she burst out.

Henry Jim looked up blankly from the funny book Leeroy had left on the table.

"Papa, I mean," Enie cried, maddened further by her brother's stupidity. "Him and that woman over yonder, with her perfume and paint and all her little tricks to nab him. He's dumb enough to fall for them, hook, line and sinker, too. You know what I'm talking about, Henry Jim Singleton. Don't make out like you haven't seen them carrying on at church!" She sat down, placing her clenched hands on the table, glaring at Henry Jim.

"I didn't say nothing," Henry Jim protested, scowling. "'So they're courtin' one another. It's no skin off your nose, is it?"

Enie swallowed desperately but the lump in her throat did not shift. She felt the disconcerting sting of tears under her lids. "That's right," she said, low and bitterly. "Take up for them. Don't give Mamma a thought. You don't care about all she did for us—for him, too, most of all! Dr. Helms as good as said that's what killed her."

"Aw, come on, Enie. You got no call to carry on so; I reckon Pa does the best he can—according to his lights."

"According to his lights. Well, let me tell you his lights are mighty dim." She jerked her shoulder toward the lamp on the table. "Just like these kerosene lamps we have to see by when most folks have electric lights and think nothing of it. He'd die before he'd listen to anybody smarter than him—anybody who knows anything. Only Miss Elsie Mae! She can come along and make him forget Mamma's slaving and scrimping all her life . ." She couldn't go on. The tears were running down her face now, falling on her hands locked in front of her on the table, and sobs choked her.

Henry Jim scowled helplessly at the comic book a moment, then raised his eyes to his weeping sister. "Look, Enie, you're all outa kilter. You can't see straight, what with feeling so bad about Mamma and all. But Pa doing without a woman the rest of his life won't bring Ma back." He began to roll the comic book tightly, his big hands torturing it, his scowl deepening. "I don't get you; way I figger it is, things would be a heap easier for you if Pa did get a wife. You could be like other girls then, have a feller yourself, and . . ."

"I don't want a fellow," Enie shouted, beating her fists on the table. You don't understand, nobody understands! Men are so . . . so . . . they don't understand anything!"

"Well, much obliged," Henry Jim retorted. "You got a mighty high opinion of us, haven't you?" But Enie ignored his heavy attempt at levity, and he leaned toward her, a little frightened now. "Look here, Enie, ain't that just the trouble? You need a woman here—to talk to and . . . and be company to you. Like Mamma used to. If Pa and Miss Elsie Mae did get married . . ."

"Don't you dare compare her to Mamma!" Enie cried, mopping at the tears she could not stop, straightening up to face Henry Jim through them. "You mean to sit there and tell me she could ever be like our mother for one single second, in one single act or work—or anything? That she wouldn't remind me how different she is from Mamma everytime I heard that whinnying laugh or watched her making Leeroy and Jenny the way she wants them and taking over the whole place to run it the way she wants it? You think I could stand that? Maybe you wouldn't mind having a stepmother come bossing you around, but I'm not going to stand for it."

"Well, what are you going to do about it?" Henry Jim shrugged, his patience waning.

Enie stared at the lamp with a dreadful stare. Her lips quivered but she did not cry again. "I don't know," she said hollowly. "I don't know."

"Maybe they don't aim to get hitched," Henry Jim offered, feebly. "Maybe Pa's just foolin' around to kill the time . . ."

"Then he ought to be ashamed," Enie said thickly. "Acting like that—and Mamma gone only a few months." She got up stiffly and went to bed, leaving Henry Jim with his comic book.

The following afternoon she saw Mr. Orin Thompson stop at the mailbox and she wandered listlessly out to see what he had left. It was a letter from T.H. addressed to Mamma. It bore an airmail stamp and had a return address in the corner in T.H.'s cramped handwriting.

Enie went into the front room and closed the door, but some moments passed before she could bring herself to open the letter. A dull anger at

T.H. stirred in her mind as she looked at the postmark and the street and number under T.H.'s name. He had got clear to Detroit, Michigan. Enie turned the wonder of it over in her mind, sitting on the side of the bed that had not been slept in since Mamma died. At last she opened the letter and read it.

"Dear Mamma," T.H. had written, *"I am sitting down to write you as it has been such a long time since I wrote last, but I had some trouble getting settled where I am and did not want to worry you. Now everything is O.K. and you will be surprised to hear what I am writing to tell you because I guess you never thought of it happening for a long time, but I am getting married Christmas Eve to a girl out here. She is a peach and I know you would approve of her."*

Enie spread the page on her knee and pressed her palm over it. T.H. getting married? In a big city up north, to a girl none of them had ever laid eyes on . . . Her surprise was dulled by distance in both time and space; she had little real feeling about it. It must be two years now since T.H. had run away. He would be twenty now, and Enie did not know when she had last thought of him— when Mamma died, probably. She took the letter up and continued reading.

"I would send a little something in this, but you can see I had to put by every cent I could spare so I can afford to take care of my wife. Guess that will strike you funny ha ha. Her name is Christine and she is sure pretty and has a good job like I have so we will make out just fine. I will close now Ma and get my sleep as I go to work on the early shift. Do not worry I have never had it so good. Your son T.H.
P.S. Sue Ann must be a big girl now and the baby not a baby any more."

Enie tucked the letter back into the envelope, took it into the kitchen and propped it against the toothpick-holder. She heard Papa hammering in the shed and thought, wryly, that he and T.H. had something in common now.

When Papa came in, Enie watched him take the letter from the table and turn it slowly in his cold hands, staring at it. Without saying anything he opened it, his lips moving over his slow reading. When he had finished he made as if to crush it in his fist, but didn't; he looked at it again and dropped it on the table.

"You best write him—now you see where he's at," he said, not looking at Enie. The bitterness in his tone found an echo in Enie's heart. "Reckon he just might be interested to know his sister and his mother have passed on. Young fool! It warn't enough to light out way up there, he's got to marry some little . . ."

"Don't you approve of *young* people marrying. Papa?"

He turned on her, his face reddening, her sarcasm wasted. "I don't approve of nothing about him," he said, "an' I don't care what he does. But *she'd* of cared. She spoke of him when she laid there at the last, said his name last of all."

Hope sprang painfully alive in Enie. She made an impulsive move toward Papa, thinking to take advantage of the memory Miss Elsie Mae had not yet destroyed. But the habit of years checked her, kept her clutching the back of the chair, the resurrected hope struggling in her eyes with contempt and fear. Papa walked to the window and stood looking into the yard, his broad, stooped back to her.

That night Enie wrote to T.H. She told him that Sue Ann and Mamma had died and were buried in Pleasant Grove churchyard, and she gave him the blessing she knew Mamma would have sent. She made no mention of Miss Elsie Mae Howells.

On Christmas morning Papa stolidly passed round the brown paper parcels, then went hunting with Henry Jim. Enie went absent-mindedly about her dinner preparations, and at about eleven o'clock Howells' car stopped at the gate. Sonny Howells stamped into the house with an armload of tissue-wrapped packages, his grin sheepish above them. 'Where 'bouts will I put these, Enie?"

And without waiting for her to answer he laid them on the table she had just covered with Mamma's neatly darned white cloth that was older than Leeroy. "Sis sent 'em—and her wishes to you all for a merry Christmas."

"Thank you kindly," Enie managed faintly, adding with sharpness, "Get back from that table, Leeroy, Jenny! You'll dirty the cloth." But the children did not heed her and crowded up, shiny-eyed with rapture. She turned to see Sonny to the door, but he had slipped away, unnoticed in the children's noisy excitement.

"Look, Enie, looka here," Leeroy screamed, flashing a brand new harmonica under her eyes. "Lookit how big it is! Must be ten more holes than my old one's got. Yippee! Lissen!' He ran a series of notes so shrill Enie had to stop her ears. Jenny squatted, spellbound, before a set of dishes too real to be true, and entirely breakable. Leeroy was shouting at Enie, "Look, look, here's yourn," pointing to the card that stuck perkily from the middle of a scarlet bow. "Ain't you goin' to open it?"

"You can if you want to," Enie muttered, raising a pot lid, wincing from the cloud of steam.

"They's something for Henry Jim, too," Leeroy announced, twitching at the bow on Enie's package. "This one here's the biggest, though, wonder what's in it. Aw, clothes!" Enie turned in spite of herself.

The skirt still lay in the box, neatly folded, soft and kitten-gray, but Leeroy held the blouse out, his hands mussing the long, full sleeves. Enie saw at a glance the little round collar, the crystal buttons winking like jewels down the front. She clattered the lid onto the pot, moved toward the table, staring down at the blouse Leeroy had dumped back into the box, to return to his harmonica.

I'll never wear it, Enie told herself, wiping her hands on her apron. She could not tear her eyes away from the satiny sheen of the blouse. Hardly knowing what she did, she lifted the gray wool skirt from the box, unfolded it. She knew Miss Elsie Mae had made it—the blouse, too—her piano-playing hands taking infinite pains with the exquisite stitches. Quickly she thrust the garments into the box and bore it away to her room. She didn't intend for Papa to see; she was never going to wear them anyway.

Clearing the table to set it, she saw the big, square envelope addressed to Mr. Clement Singleton. Enie was not fooled; all the Christmas gifts were for Papa. For his attention, his gratitude. Enie placed Henry Jim's unopened present and Papa's card on the shelf and began to set the table. When she heard the men's voices in the yard she set the food on the table.

Enie didn't mean to look at Papa when he opened the envelope, but her eyes flew to his face as he drew the card from the envelope—a life-size poinsettia and writing she could not make out, of course. She saw the flush stain his fleshy jowls as he laid the card back on the shelf. She saw Henry

Jim looking straight and hard at her, his ready-made bow tie in his hand, and she heard herself saying loudly, "She gave me a blouse and skirt. My clothes may be shoddy, but I don't need new ones that bad."

"Set down," Papa ordered sternly. "Vittles are gettin' cold."

While Papa was galloping through grace Enie saw Henry Jim making a hideous face at her. She wanted, unreasonably, to cry as the food began its rapid passage from plate to plate.

Toward evening the rain that had threatened all day began to fall. It veiled the horizon in a gray mist and fogged the windowpanes. Papa smoked his pipe, then got a tangled ball of string from the table drawer and began to unknot it, his hands clumsy and painstaking. Enie wondered if he were thinking of Mamma—or Miss Elsie Mae. Not one of them had mentioned Mamma's name all day. As she watched, brooding, he surprised her by saying, "Better git to bed. You musta had a hard day, fixin' that good dinner. Hit was real good, your ma herself couldn't hardly have cooked a hen better."

Enie lighted the other lamp and took it to her room. She opened the box that contained Miss Elsie Mae's gift, her roughened fingers catching at the soft silk of the blouse. The gem-bright buttons winked in the lamplight. She laid the blouse over a chair back and unfolded the skirt, held it against her. It wouldn't hurt to try it on—just to see if it fitted. That didn't mean she would wear it any-where—ever.

She got out of her old dress and slipped the skirt over her head. It was a tiny bit too big in the waist, not enough to hurt. Its fullness fell softly about her thin hips; the length was exactly right. She put the blouse on and tucked it in; it was a perfect fit. How had Miss Elsie Mae—with never a chick or child to sew for—known her exact size? She took her graduation pumps from under the bed and put them on. Moving the lamp closer to the mirror, she looked at herself and thought, I wish Mamma could see me now. Or Ralph Shane . . .

She walked several times back and forth across the room, her young girl's starved heart going out to the new clothes. As stylish as the town girls'. She looked every bit as elegant as Mary Lee Williams. If she wore the new outfit to church next preaching Sunday there would be many admiring looks sent her way—among them Miss Elsie Mae's. Well, she wasn't going to wear them. Not ever.

Her hands shook with anger as she shoved the box into one end of the drawer and tried to close it. It stuck and she gave it a kick that made Jenny jabber something in her sleep. Enie wriggled into her nightgown and blew out the light. She shoved Jenny and the new baby doll over so she could settle in beside them.

18

—————

AFTER THE FIRST of the year Papa went three nights a week to court Miss Elsie Mae.

Enie watched helplessly; there was nothing she could do or say. It would take an act of God to stop it now and God was not on Enic's side. Sometimes she felt, miserably, that *Mamma* was not on her side; her rudeness to Miss Elsie Mae, her resentment and her hate were not things Mamma would ever have condoned. She kept her stubborn vow not to wear the skirt and blouse Miss Elsie Mae had given her for Christmas, though they tempted her every Saturday when she dressed to go to town. Angry and frightened, she saw the winter days pass and spring come again to Tired Creek.

It was the last Saturday night in April that Papa told Enie,

She was doing the supper dishes. Papa walked twice round the table and cleared his throat loudly before Enie turned and looked at him. He looked hot and uncomfortable in his blue serge suit; he had shaved so close that the skin of his face was blotched, and the unruly waves of his red hair lay dark from the wet comb.

"I reckon you ought to know." Papa said stiltedly, "I intend to make Miss Elsie Mae Howells my wife. I'd not want it to come to you from ary other source." He was obliged to clear his throat again. "Still, I don't reckon it hardly comes as a surprise." He clasped his hands behind him and bent his head. "I have give it a heap of studying—and I think it's the thing to do." He waited expectantly and when Enie said nothing he went on, dignified as a preacher, "I figger a suitable time has passed since your mamma was taken from our midst."

"It's less than a year since Mamma died," Enie said then, coldly.

"An' I haven't made no second marriage yet, either. She . . . We haven't settled on a time, but likely it will be this summer. Miss Elsie Mae is a good, Christian woman. She would not show disrespect to your mamma's memory."

"Wouldn't she?" Enie didn't even think whether or not she was "sassing" Papa. But he flushed vividly.

"I need me somebody here in my home to raise my younguns."

"What about me?" Enie asked dully. "Haven't I

been raising them like Mamma wanted? Like she asked me to?"

"Now hold your horses, Miss," Papa commanded. "You got no call to carry on. You've done real good an' I'm obliged to you for givin' me no trouble an' doin' your part like your mamma's daughter that you are. But I aim to marry with Miss Elsie Mae like I said, an' I don't want no monkeyshines cut over it." He picked his hat from the table, opened the door and walked out.

As from an immeasurable distance the children's high voices drifted in from the yard. Henry Jim's footsteps came down the hall, passed the door and crossed the back porch. Enie moved to the window and saw the pickup truck backing out of the barn. She went back to her dishwashing and worked mechanically till she had finished. She hung her sacking apron on the nail behind the door and sat down with her hands stretched out before her; their pink puckered palms seemed to stare up at her, telling their own story. The window was blue with dusk, the kitchen shrouded in dimness, but she made no move to light the lamp. She was trying to imagine Miss Elsie Mae Howells in this kitchen, this room where Mamma had worked her life out without rebellion or complaint.

The door creaked inward and the children took shape in the rectangle of twilight. She could feel their eyes picking her out in the dimness, feel their uneasiness wavering toward her. "How come you don't light the light, Enie?" Leeroy asked, and Jenny added, "It's dark in here."

Enie stirred. "You can light the lamp if you want to, Leeroy," she said. Leeroy groped for matches on the stove shelf, Jenny crept in and stood near Enie. Pale yellow light flickered over the room, leaving the corners in shadow. Leeroy replaced the chimney and adjusted the wick to stop its smoking. He and Jenny looked at Enie with the steady, relentless gaze of children.

"What you crying for?" Leeroy demanded. When Enie did not answer they looked at each other. Jenny's face crumpled but Leeroy scowled. He had grown a lot taller, this year, but he was as scrawny as ever, his shoulder blades still like wings. As his eyes went from Jenny's puckered face to Enie's bowed head, a wildness gathered like a sudden storm in their depths. With a vehement motion he seized the sugar bowl that sat inoffensively in the middle of the table and dashed it to the floor.

Horror dried the tears in Jenny's eyes. Enie raised her head and wiped her face with the back of her hand. She looked without comment at the wreckage on the floor.

"You've broke it," Jenny wailed. "You've broke the sugar bowl."

"Never mind," Enie sighed pushing her hair back "He couldn't help it."

The unexpected kindness cracked Leeroy's armor. His face twisted and he went down on his knees to gather the bits of crockery. Jenny, afraid of being left out of whatever was happening, ran to get the broom; silently the three cleared away the litter. When Enie poured the little pile of sugar into the big bucket Jenny watched with interest, but Leeroy turned away. With a steady hand Enie turned the lamp wick a little higher. "You'll all go to bed now," she said, and they gave her no argument.

Enie found Henry Jim hanging over the lot fence. Something in his attitude told her he was deep in thought—a rare procedure for Henry Jim.

"Did Papa tell you?" she asked. Henry Jim whistled softly a tune he'd got from Seedy Culpepper.

"What's to tell? I been knowing all along, same as you."

"You don't care," Enie accused, "but I . . ."

"Look," Henry Jim broke in nervously, "had you thought about it might mean you could go off to school like you wanted to?"

"On *her* money? I wouldn't do that, not if I never know anything!"

"All right, if you have to be so stuck-up about everything. Mamma wanted you to go, didn't she?"

"Maybe Mamma wanted to live, too," Enie said. She began to tremble. "Listen to me, Henry Jim. I haven't had a chance to think it out or anything, but what if you and I could make a deal of some kind—things won't be the same with Papa, they can't!—and if Pa would pay us a share, you and me . . ." She had to stop her rush of words to swallow, and Henry Jim's laugh kept her from going on.

"Share-croppers. That'd be a swell thing for you, wouldn't it?"

"If I got paid I could put it into my education. It would be money I earned myself."

"Aw, you're nuts, it wouldn't work—even if Pa'd agree to it. And he wouldn't, you know Papa."

"Yes," Enie said in a voice gone flat and hopeless, "I know Papa." She let her body sag against the lot fence, her nostrils suddenly full of the faintly sour scent of the pigpen on the other side of the lot. She knew Henry Jim was right, that she'd only clutched at a straw. He was talking now and the animation in his tone told her he was looking toward his own big chance.

"I reckon Pa means for me and Son Howells all to work both farms—theirs and ours. Ought to be a pretty good deal—with all the equipment they've got over there and all. With three able-bodied men and all that machinery it'd be crazy to take a girl on."

"Forget it." Enie muttered.

Every day Enie looked for Miss Elsie Mae to come

and add her effervescent say to Papa's announcement, but she did not appear. She's got what she was after, Enie told herself then. There's no need for presents and petting now. School was out, the anniversary of Mamma's death came and went, an the family went about its business as always. Enie said nothing to Leeroy or Jenny of what portended and Papa and Henry Jim were as little disposed to talk with her as she was to them.

It was not a Monday, but Enie, too restless to settle to anything, made Leeroy fire the washpots after breakfast and was hanging the first line of wash when Miss Elsie Mac said cheerfully behind her, "I'll help you hang 'em. Then we can have us a little talk while the menfolks are out of the way."

Enie's fingers thrust the clothespin so violently over Henry Jim's drawers that the worn fabric ripped and she heard Miss Elsie Mae's rueful clucking as the white hands went busily into the grocery carton for the next garment. "Papa told me," she said harshly, not looking at Miss Elsie Mae.

Miss Elsie May whipped Jenny's apron briskly, fastened it to the line and gave her nervous giggle. "I know he did. But I been wanting to talk to you a right smart while, Enie. Womenfolks need it more than men, I reckon."

Enie maintained a stony silence. If Miss Elsie Mae thought she could soft-soap her into coming around at this late date, she had another think coming. She tried to hide her agitation, but her water-puckered fingers were clumsy, dropping a pin, slowing her down so that her helper made twice as good time as she did, and the damp cardboard box was empty before she had disposed of more than a handful of pieces.

"I won't hold you up long," Miss Elsie Mae said placatingly as she followed Enie round the house to the porch. The warm scent of chinaberry blossoms drifted to the porch and Enie grudgingly pushed a chair to the shady side. She watched with hard eyes as Miss Elsie Mae settled herself. "Sit down, honey. What I got to say won't take but a minute or two."

Enie lowered herself to the edge of a straight chair, seeing out of the sides of her eyes the reproachful emptiness of Mamma's rocker at the other end of the porch. Beyond the gate Leeroy's and Jenny's voices rose happily from the interior of Sonny Howells' car. Enie opened her mouth to call to them, but Miss Elsie Mae put a hand on the thin knee jutting sharply beneath Enie's faded skirt. "Let 'em be. I told them they could play in the car." She chuckled. "Look at that Leeroy behind the wheel! Bet he thinks he's halfway to Andalusia." But when Enie did not smile, she sighed and drew her hand away.

"Papa told me you all were aiming to get married," Enie said, looking down at her old sneakers.

"That's right. I'm bound to say you don't act

like it was good news," Miss Elsie Mae said in a subdued voice. "But you'll see we can be a real happy family if you give us a chance, Earline."

"When are you and Papa going to—get married?"

"We thought next preaching Sunday. Brother Dix will be out here, save him a trip. It's not the time of year to be taking time off, your papa's too busy. What's the sense of it, anyhow?" Enie, glancing up in spite of herself, saw color flooding Miss Elsie Mae's face, though she held her chin high and proud. "There's not going to be any nonsense about my wedding, that's one of the things I wanted to tell you. Your father is a plain man, a fine man too. Oh, I know his rough talk and strict ways, but they don't mean a thing to me!" A secret smile lifted the corners of her lips. "I think a heap of your dad, Enie, I sure do."

Enie looked at her bare legs stretched in front of her. A fly crawled tantalizingly along one of them but she let him be, perversely savoring the affliction. "Next preaching Sunday is the one after this coming one," she said.

"That's right. I thought we could just have Brother Dix stay a few minutes after the service and perform the ceremony right there in the church house."

So she wasn't going to have it in the fine parlor with the silk-shaded lamp and the radio, no feast in the nice dining room with the fine furniture. The breeze died and the chinaberry leaves were still—swooning in their own sweetness. An old Dominick hen wallowed with delight in a dusthole she had scratched out for herself.

"I wouldn't care," Enie broke out hoarsely, "if it was just Henry Jim and me. But Leeroy and Jenny —they're so little. They're used to me. They might not understand me not being the one to . . ."

"Now don't you go to worrying about those little old younguns, Enie. They'll make out the best in the world with me, you just see if they don't. Why, Leeroy and Jenny like me fine already!"

"I know they do," Enie admitted, sullenly. "You made them like you because you wanted to get Papa. You went to a lot of trouble to make them like you. You thought of everything—except Mamma being gone such a little while."

At Miss Elsie Mae's sharp intake of breath Enie raised her eyes. Miss Elsie Mae's face seemed to have shrunk under the tirade, its usually camouflaged lines standing out bold and ugly like a betrayal. She rose slowly, uncertainly from her chair, as if her limbs too had suddenly grown older.

"I didn't know it was that bad with you," she said, moving toward the steps. "I'll be going." She hesitated then, turned, searching Enie's mutinous face with a pitying look. A little cry escaped her and she came near, not taking her eyes from Enie. "You poor child, you. I reckon it's only natural for you to feel so. Your mother was a good woman, don't think I don't know that. A better woman than I am, I know that, too. I can't believe she'd begrudge your papa a woman to take care of him. And wouldn't your mamma, if she could speak out and say so, be glad of a mother's love and care for her little children she was obliged to leave?"

"I've given them love and care," Enie cried, knowing she was taking a last hopeless stand. "Nobody can say I haven't kept my word to Mamma to look after Leeroy and Jenny!"

Miss Elsie Mae nodded vigorously. "You're right, Enie, you sure have taken good care of them. But you're just a young girl, you're one of your mother's children, too. You ought not to be saddled with cares like an old woman! Many a time my heart has ached for you these months past . . ."

"You don't need to be sorry for me—or any of us," Enie said, but a growing confusion made it difficult for her to talk back to Miss Elsie Mae.

"Enie," Miss Elsie Mae said then, so solemnly and quietly that Enie trembled as she did when Brother Dix held the revivals at Pleasant Grove Church, "if you are worried about Leeroy and Jenny—if you think I could be mean to them—I can set your mind to rest. I will swear to you here and now on your mother's Holy Bible that I will be good to them, that I will be a mother to them as if they'd been born to me. I'll swear that on the Book if you'll go get it."

Looking Miss Elsie Mae in the eye because she could not help herself, feeling a little sick at the significance of the words falling humbly yet with such awful solemnity from her lips, Enie felt as if she were seeing Miss Elsie Mae Howells for the first time. For the first time she was seeing the honest, the humble, the *good* Miss Elsie Mae, who till this moment, had been hidden behind the silly laugh, the roving eye, the loud, cheerful, irritating dominance. "Go on, honey, get your mamma's Bible."

"No, ma'am, I'll take your word. You don't have to swear on the Book. It's only—" she threw Miss Elsie Mae a look of desperation—"I didn't *want* anyone in Mamma's place. I wanted them to remember their own mother. Maybe Jenny's already forgot—she's not but five."

Miss Elsie Mae took one of Enie's hands, squeezed it and slowly released it. "What if she has forgot, Enie? She's just made a little start on her life, all of it before her yet, please God. Like it says in the burial service, death is always in the midst of life—but it's the living that have to live and make the best job of it they can. Jenny won't forget her mamma any quicker with a little extra love. And if it's any comfort to you—not that I'm bragging, Enie—she and Leeroy will have it easier lots of ways than you older children have. I don't claim to be rich, but I'm fixed comfortable and it'll give me pure pleasure to share what the good Lord's seen fit to bless me with. Share it with all of you—if you'll just unbend a little bit and put your trust in me."

218

The silence hung heavy between them for a moment, then Miss Elsie Mae sighed, went down the walk and through the gate. With her hand on the door of the car she turned and called to Enie, "I'll take Leeroy and Jenny home with me if you don't mind. Give you a little while to yourself to get done with that washing I interrupted." Enie nodded, unable to speak for the dreadful need to cry.

As she pounded the wet clothes on the top of the oak stump with the battling stick worn paper-smooth by the years of Mamma's wielding, the tears ran freely down Enie's face. With the sweat of her labor they slipped quietly over her cheeks, leaving an emptiness that was almost peace to spread within her. It was as if she had let Miss Elsie Mae take along with Jenny and Leeroy the hate and anger, the horrid dog-in-the-manger thing she had mistaken for loyalty to Mamma. She wept for many things: for Mamma's death, for Jenny and Leeroy whom, in a sense, she had already given over to Miss Elsie Mae; she wept for shame of her own unworthiness. She cried till she had no more tears, then washed her face and combed her hair and prepared the midday dinner.

All the long, hot afternoon she kept recalling Miss Elsie Mae's words, a dim familiarity worrying at the edge her mind. It was not till just before she slept that night that the answer broke with clarity in her circling thoughts. Miss Elsie Mae had talked like Mamma.

19

ENIE WAS ON HER HANDS and knees scrubbing the kitchen floor when she heard voices just outside the window. Peeking cautiously over the sill she saw Papa and Mr. Tom Shane. They stood talking for a moment, gesturing in the slow, spacious manner of farmers, then walked toward the west field. As she was throwing the last rinse water onto the petunia bed Papa came through the house, got his hat and drove off with Mr. Tom in his car. About four o'clock the big car stopped long enough to let Papa out at the gate. Enie heard him, a little later, bumbling about in the bedroom, then he came into the kitchen where Enie was indifferently getting things together for supper.

Papa stood looking at Enie as if he had not seen her for a long time, and she noticed that he held his bankbook in his hand, gingerly—as if he were afraid of it. "He's got it. That piece he's hankered after these many years. I sold him my west field."

Enic looked at him, stupefied. "You sold your field to Mr. Shane? What for?"

Papa slapped the bankbook sharply against his palm. "For money. That's what for. And he's like a bull. He'd never give an inch an' all the time smilin' that easy way all the Shanes do when he never aimed to back down ary bit!"

"But you wouldn't give an inch either, all those years! You said you'd never sell. I must've heard you a hundred times, Papa."

"Yeah, you must've heard me that many times, easy. I said it and meant it. I never aimed to let him get aholt of that land."

"Then . . . why . . ."

"He come up on his price. Looked like he didn't care what he paid long as he got his way. Set his head on some special kind of experi-ment with it, he said. Raised his price till I'd just natcherly of been a fool to turn him down." But Papa wasn't coming clean. Enie could tell he was holding back something; she thought it was his real reason for the sale he had vowed he would never make.

"Did you need the money real bad?"

"You ever seen a time when I didn't need money? You ought to know how a farm eats up money, let alone kids to raise and sickness and such. Then, when there's a big expense like sending a young one off to school . . ."

The blood sprang in a painful tide to Enie's face, then drained away leaving it pale and her lips dry. "Do you mean me, Papa? You're aiming to send me to college, after all?"

They stared at each other, then Papa drew his sleeve across his face. "Howells' farm is four-five times the size of this. I reckoned I could spare a few acres—where I couldn't of, before."

"Did Miss Elsie Mae talk you into selling your land, Papa?"

"No. No, she never talked me into nothing. I make up my own mind, I thank you, always have and always will." He chewed savagely at his lip and when he went on his voice had gentled unbelievably. "It was *her* that wanted it. You know that was what she wanted from the time you younguns out here all commenced boarding that bus and ridin' to the town school. Only I couldn't see my way to it before. Things—have changed, now."

"Yes, sir," Enie said, huskily, "they sure have." She pretended to squint at a splinter in her finger. "Will you—will we live in Howells' house then, after you and Miss Elsie Mae get married?"

Papa nodded slowly. "It's a better house, bigger, more room. An' there's her brother she's looked after all these years . . . It seems like the best thing to do, us go there. It's not like we was a pair of dead beats, me and Henry Jim. I reckon we'll carry our weight." He fidgeted with the bankbook, then raised his head. "Anyhow, Tom Shane's buyin' this house. Says he's got a tenant with a big family, needs a place right off quick. I don't know if I done the right thing—selling the house like that. But it looks like it. With all the extry I'm taking on an' two men workin' with me—looks like we ought to do pretty good." He was looking out the window now and Enie saw something in his face she had never seen there before; it was hope, strong and alive.

Enie let her gaze follow Papa's out the window; she saw a bit of back yard, the fence Seedy Culpepper had helped to build, a corner of the woodshed where T.H. had taken his last whipping, Jenny's dark head bobbing over her mud pies. Everything was going to be different. Different and better for them all. Only—why had Mamma had to die for it to be?

Papa opened the table drawer and laid his little book in it. Enie went over and timidly caught his sleeve. "I'll do my best, Papa, so the money won't be wasted, I promise. And—I'll pay it back as soon as I can, like I said before."

Papa drew his arm from her fingers, but not roughly. He looked only as if he had had enough of an embarrassing situation and wanted to escape. "No hurry about it," he mumbled. "Might be you'd have to take care of me in my helpless old age."

On Saturday, when Papa parked the pickup in front of People's Grocery Store, Enie handed her grocery list to Henry Jim. "I'm obliged to tend to a little business," she said. "I'll try not to be long." And when Henry Jim started to protest, she turned to Leeroy. "You keep Jenny right with you, hear? If you're good I might get you some candy when I get back." Leeroy, who wanted to look at bicycles at the hardware store, scowled and Enie hurriedly produced a dime. "Get you and Jenny a drink," she coaxed, and Leeroy went off toward Williams' Pharmacy with Jenny trotting after him.

Papa had already disappeared into the dimness of the grocery store and Enie walked down Main Street, trying to appear dignified and calm and as if she knew exactly how to go about what she had to do. She turned the corner into Academy Street where the schoolhouse stood in vacation loneliness, its playground already invaded by weeds. She didn't allow her steps to lag, though the knot of nerves in her stomach tried to slow her down. She saw Mr. Claye's house squatting in a half-acre of shabby Bermuda grass. She let herself pause at the two tall sycamores guarding the gate only long enough for a deep breath, then went up the walk and across the porch.

Mrs. Claye, a small, sandy woman with a harassed expression, answered Enie's timid knock on the screen door. A smell of bacon from breakfast drifted through the hall.

"I wanted to see Mr. Claye if he's at home," Enie requested, responding to Mrs. Claye's smile with a nervous one of her own.

Mrs. Claye held the door open. "You come right in and have a seat. He's just stepped out to the garden." She showed Enie into a living room so crowded with shabby furniture, so lined with books, so choked with bric-a-brac that Enie dared not move for fear of knocking something over. She eased herself into a chair and stared at the books whose titles she could not read for her tense preoccupation. She heard Mrs. Claye's voice shrilling, "Hor-ace, oh, Hor-ace!"

In a moment Mr. Claye appeared, incongruously clad in overalls at least a size too big for him. "Well, well, Earline!" He grasped Enie's hand and shook it. "You must excuse my appearance. I was just getting around to a little gardening. Sit down," he urged, for Enie had risen at his entrance. "I am glad to see you. How are things out Tired Creek way?" He drew a chair toward Enie's. "Another year has gone and we've loosed another flock of graduates upon the world. One can't help wondering what sort of world, I'm sorry to say."

Enie gratefully seized the proffered cue. "That's what I came to see you about, Mr. Claye. I'm going out into the world, too. I'm going to college."

Light suffused Mr. Claye's face. "Why, I am delighted to hear that, Earline! I remember your fine record. I can't tell you how happy I am to know you're going back to school next fall."

"I don't want to wait till fall," Enie explained quickly. "I want to go to summer school if it's not too late to get in. I—I can get away from home now, and I thought you could tell me what to do."

Mr. Claye was all business at once. He reached for a calendar that stood crookedly on the cluttered desk. "I believe June seventeenth is registration day at Mills. I was looking over their catalog only this week."

Enie nodded. "That's where I aim—plan to go, sir. What do I have to do to get in?"

"Why, I'll be glad to write to the office of the registrar if you'd like," Mr. Claye offered. "I'll send a transcription of your credits and you'll be sent the necessary forms to fill in. You can mail it back or take it along with you if time should run short. I believe fees are payable upon registration. I can't tell you how glad I am you can go without further delay."

"That's mighty nice of you, Mr. Claye. I'm surely obliged to you." Blushing, Enie stood up and Mr. Claye rose also, shaking her hand again, his kindly smile dissolving the knot inside her, making her feel for the first time a sense of reality in the whole strange business she had undertaken.

"Not at all, Earline, not at all. Glad to be of any help. If you should run into any difficulty—which you won't, I'm sure—don't hesitate to come to me. I'm sure you'll be a credit to Green Pine school and to Tired Creek community."

That night, when Papa set out after supper to pay his call on Miss Elsie Mae, Enie followed him to the truck. "Can I talk to you a minute, Papa?"

she asked, feeling every bit as nervous as she had at Mr. Claye's house.

Papa climbed into the cab of the truck but did not start the motor. In the dwindling daylight his eyes were very blue and wary, a "what now" look in them.

"I saw Mr. Claye in town today. I asked him about entering summer school at Mills Falls. I don't want to wait till September, I've lost a whole year already. It starts the seventeenth. I—I'm not sure what the tuition comes to . . ." She faltered. "I'm afraid it's a lot—a hundred dollars or more."

Papa winced, pushed his hat up and scratched his head consideringly. Enie began to feel hollow inside; was Papa going to change his mind at the mention of so much cash money? After all, how far was it possible for a man to depart from his nature? "I aim to work after I get there. Lots of students help pay their way."

"M-m-m. I don't see nothing wrong with that. But it ain't only the money . . ." Enie felt his embarrassment reaching toward her; he did not meet her eyes. "I didn't look for none of it to be cheap. I'm thinking it won't look right, you pulling off from the rest of your folks just when this change is made."

"Oh, Papa, everybody knows I've been wanting to go away to school." She had a flash of inspiration and used it. "Miss Elsie Mae especially! She'll understand, I know—just like Mamma would."

The old pain of loyalty flared sharply and subsided, swallowed in the quiet resignation of her next words. "You tell her tonight, or I will if you want me to."

Papa rubbed his thumb along the broken door of the truck. Enie sensed his wariness changing to the helpless acceptance of women and their inscrutable ways for which a hard-working man had no time. He opened the door, slammed and fastened it with its baling-wire device, shoved his thumb down on the starter button. "I'll get the money for you Saturday," he promised over the coughing of the motor.

"Yes, sir. Thank you, Papa," Enie had to shout, thrusting her face over the vibrating door.

All the nervous energy which had kept her going since he'd told of his sale of the land seemed to go out of the yard with the rattling pickup truck. She stood where it had left her, fingering her apron, thinking emptily how much there still was to do. But she was bone-tired all of a sudden, fit for nothing but to fall into bed. Tomorrow she could pick up where she'd left off and go ahead.

20

THERE WERE MOMENTS when time passed so swiftly it frightened Enie; others when it seemed to stand still and she would stop in the middle of some chore she had started, merely to impede her thoughts and listen for the reassuring tick of the cracked clock. She had Henry Jim bring Mamma's little humpbacked tin trunk out of the shed before the middle of the week—though an hour would have provided time for packing of her possessions. She had not told Jenny what was going to happen, and after each of her brief packing bouts she pushed the trunk under her bed.

Sometimes she felt frantic, trying to keep in mind all that must be done to terminate neatly her life here in this house that now belonged to Mr. Tom Shane. She would long for the week to be over, for all the painful things to be done and the new life begun. A letter came from the office of the registrar at Mills College confirming the date of registration and enclosing a bewildering form full of questions to be answered. Holding the letter in her hand, Enie knew a moment of sheer exultation, a moment in which all was forgotten except the fact that her chance had come at last. She wanted to run down the road and shout the truth to all Tired Creek. Later she thought she might as well have done so, for Tired Creek knew before the week was out.

Miss Sadie Hightower came to wish Enie well and say how happy Mamma would have been. Carol Vance brought a tatting-edged handkerchief, her face plainly showing her incredulity that anyone with twelve years of school behind her could voluntarily start such a grind again. Nevertheless, her "Good luck, Enie" was ungrudging and sincere. Miss Katy Powell sent word by Leeroy that Enie was to come to the store if she could catch a lift, and on Thursday Enie walked the long way, scarcely noticing the heat. Miss Katy laid a pink rayon slip with a deep border of lace on Enie's lap.

"I hope it's the right size," she worried, flicking at an infinitesimal speck. "I asked Lou Addie when she was by here and she said a thirty-two."

Enie had to blink tears from her eyes before she could thank Miss Katy, who brushed the thanks aside. "You been such a good girl and had such a hard year you sure deserve your turn." Enie was certain Miss Elsie Mae had given out the news; Papa was such a stickler for minding his business and keeping it to himself. "Your papa will have it easier now, too, won't he? I'm glad for him."

Watching good little spinster Miss Katy wrap the slip in brown paper—not forgetting to enclose a sack of jawbreakers—Enie had a moment of panic; in a few days she would be leaving these people to go among strangers into a strange world.

She was still turning the awesome thought over in her mind when she heard the motor behind her and stepped out of the sandy rut without looking behind her. Ralph Shane brought his father's pickup to a stop. "Want a lift, Enie? It's a hot day for such a long walk." A heifer calf, undernourished and rough-coated, was tethered in the back of the truck. It bawled piteously and braced its wobbly legs. "Poor critter," Ralph said, following Enie's curious look. "I rescued it from Thad Atkins." He closed the door as Enie settled herself beside him. "Maybe I'll have no better luck, but I bought her to try." He put the truck in low gear and drove slowly, trying to spare the calf as much discomfort as possible. "If she shapes up into a decent cow I'll take her back to him."

"You paid for her, but if you raise her you'll give her back to Thaddy?"

Ralph grinned sheepishly. "Why not. They're needy. I guess I really wanted to see if I *could* pull the poor thing through. Jimmy Hightower will give me a hand. He should have been a vet, that fellow, the way he's got with sick animals." Enie felt sure Ralph was talking to cover his compassion. She turned her face aside so he would not see her small, womanly smile.

The truck crawled along through the sand and Enie said suddenly through the calf's bawling, "I'm going away, Ralph."

"You are? Where to?" His eyes were on the road, though of course he knew every inch of it by heart.

"I'm going to Mills Falls to college."

"Why, Enie, that's swell," Ralph said. "When?"

"Early Monday morning." She looked at the parcel on her knees. "Papa and Miss Elsie Mae Howells are getting married Sunday after preaching."

"I'd heard about that," Ralph admitted. "Don't know who told me, now. But I didn't know your big news. I'm glad it was you told me."

Warmed by Ralph's words, Enie grew bold enough to speak out to Ralph this once—this last chance she might ever get—as if he were not a Shane, as if he were merely the good friend he had shown himself to be more than once. "I couldn't have gone; even if Mamma had lived, I couldn't. There wasn't any money and Papa was against it. He wouldn't have sold the land and the house to your father if he hadn't been going to marry Miss Elsie Mae Howells." She tried to laugh then, but it was something of a failure. "I was thinking it's really *your* father sending me to college."

Ralph smiled, not taking his eyes from the road. "I'd call that sort of farfetched. But the important thing is you're getting to go. It won't be wasted on you like it is on some kids, that's for sure." And again the warm, good feeling flashed through Enie.

They were approaching the lane that led to Shanes' outbuildings and she said, "You can let me off here, Ralph." But he did not stop.

"It's still a long, hot walk; I'll take you the rest of the way."

Enie turned to look through the rear window at the calf, maintaining its balance with staggering difficulty. "Poor little old thing," she said softly, seeing the beast through Ralph's eyes, an object of pity, yet fortunate too as the object of Ralph's concern. "I bet it lives and makes a fine milk cow for Atkins' hungry little kids."

"I'll remember that, Enie, for luck."

There was no sign of Papa about the place and Enie was relieved; it would be a pity to have a row so near her day of liberation. Without a scene to mar it she could take Ralph's friendliness away with her, a sort of parting gift, like the handkerchief and the pink slip. She stepped off the high running board, holding her parcel tenderly. "I'm much obliged for the ride," she told Ralph and, free forever of little-girl shyness with him, she put her hand up for Ralph to shake.

"Good-by, Enie, and the best of luck."

"Gook luck to you, too," Enie said, still feeling the warm pressure of his hand on hers after he had released it. "I hope the little calf does fine. I know she will!"

Standing by the gate, watching him turn the truck round and drive back toward home, she felt a heaviness creep under the excitement of going-away preparations and the receiving of gifts. She stared through the slowly settling dust till a voice chanted over her in a twangy singsong, "Enie's got a *fell*-er," and a chinaberry landed with a tiny hard thump on the top of her head. She jerked a startled face up to see Leeroy crouched in the branches above, grinning diabolically.

"Leeroy Singleton! You like to scared me out of my skin. Wait till I get my hands on you!"

"What's in the package?" Leeroy demanded, keeping his distance. "Ralph give it to you? If he's your feller, he . . ."

"Hush up, Leeroy. What's the matter with you? Ralph Shane's not anybody's feller. You get down out of that tree this minute."

Leeroy gripped a branch, dangled a moment, let go of the branch to dangle again. "Pa's Miss Elsie Mae's feller," he said, pert and knowing, swaying low enough now to touch Enie's head with his foot if he choose to. "An' you know what, Enie? They're gonna get married. Papa and Miss Elsie Mae."

Enie opened the gate, came into the yard, her

parcel clamped under her arm. Leeroy landed on all fours beside her.

"Where's Jenny? You promised to keep your eye on her. She might be down at the branch or off in the woods for all you know." She added anxiously, "Did you tell her—what you said just now about Papa and Miss Elsie Mae?"

Leeroy stood up, moving nimbly beyond Enie's reach, shook his head. "Naw, she's too little."

"Who told you?"

"Nobody. I been knowin' a long time. I whupped Jenks Hightower the other day, though, that day Pa sent me after the well rope. I laid him flat out in that road."

"Why?"

" 'Cause he joshed about me goin' to have a new mamma. I like Miss Elsie Mae fine—but she ain't goin' to be my mamma."

Enie's eyes filled, her impatience with Leeroy gone. "That's right, Leeroy," she said, gently. "But Miss Elsie Mae will be good to you. She promised me she would."

"Sure, she's O.K. What's in the package, Enie?"

"I'll show you if you'll find Jenny and tell her to come in. You too. I want to talk to you both."

She went slowly up the walk, casting about in her mind for words with which to tell Jenny she was going away. She told the children to wash while she built her supper fire, still feverishly wondering how she would begin.

When she had done with the fire and Leeroy and Jenny stood expectantly before her, she sat down and pulled Jenny onto her lap. Leeroy stood by, his eyes darting from Enie to the parcel on the table. It was almost milking time and Papa and Henry Jim would be coming from the field. The heaviness still lay in Enie's breast, but she made her voice bright with promise, reminding Jenny of Miss Elsie Mae's goodness, forcing herself because from long habit it still went against the grain.

She saw the two faces light up with anticipation at the prospect of going to live at Miss Elsie Mae's house with the piano and the radio. "You see," she threw in quickly, laying her cheek against Jenny's silky head, "I won't be there. Not right at first, because I'm going off to school."

"You said you was all done with school," Jenny accused. "You're too big to go to school."

"This is a school for big people," Enie explained. "I'm going there to learn to teach school myself. Think of that, Jenny, me, a schoolteacher!"

"Gee," Leeroy said, impressed for all his superiority over Jenny.

"You could take me with you," Jenny quavered, but Leeroy put in helpfully, "Aw shucks, Jenny, you wouldn't have no fun at some old college. At Miss Elsie Mae's you'll have the best time. I bet she'll let you make a little bitty cake every time she makes one of them good old big ones."

Enie hastened to back Leeroy. "I bet she will,

too, Jenny. Besides, I won't be going till time for you all to go over there. This time you won't be going for a little old visit, you're going to live at Miss Elsie Mae's. It'll be your house!"

"Leeroy's too?"

"Leeroy's too, and Henry Jim's and Papa's."

"An' ol' Minnie an' the pups an' Snowball too, huh, Enie?" Leeroy pranced around the room, forgetting the package on the table.

"Everybody but Enie," Jenny mourned softly, her brown fingers pleating a fold of Enie's skirt.

"Oh, I'll be there sometime," Enie promised, not quite believing it. "But not right at first. It'll be grand, you just wait and see. You'll have so much to do and such nice new places to play. You—you love Miss Elsie Mae, you know you do—and she loves you and Leeroy, too."

"Can I carry all my stuff over there?"

"Of course. Your big doll and your little baby and all your dishes and things. You won't take on about me not going, will you, because that will spoil everything and make me feel awful bad?" She told Leeroy to hand her the package then and showed them the slip Miss Katy had given her, and divided the jawbreakers between them. It was done and Jenny had not cried.

It was Enie who wept. After the children were asleep and she lay with her legs feeling twitchy and her eyes refusing to stay closed.

After church the next morning Enie climbed down from the truck, glancing at her dress to see if she had got grease on it. Old Minnie trotted round the corner of the house. The sun picked spaces in the yard beyond the trees. Flies buzzed round the lot. Nothing was changed, yet so much was changed.

"I thought we was goin' to Howells'," Leeroy began whiningly. "Pa and Miss Elsie Mae went with the preacher."

"Tomorrow, Leeroy," Enie said, avoiding Henry Jim's eye. "They'll come get you and Jenny tomorrow, early."

Leeroy gathered a handful of pebbles and went toward the woods. Jenny consented to taking a nap at Enie's urging. "Just till it cools down, honey." She let Enie skin her dress over her head and crawled onto the bed in her petticoat.

Henry Jim slogged self-consciously off down the road, destination unannounced, and Enie went to the branch and slipped behind the willows. She sat on the rock a long time, listening to the murmur of the water. She thought fleetingly of Seedy Culpepper, but the thought was blurred, her mind filled with nearer, more pressing things.

"Funny," she said aloud, touching a willow frond, "I don't hate Miss Elsie Mae. I don't even hate Papa any more."

She closed her eyes, savoring the peace of no longer hating. The burden had begun to ease from her the day Miss Elsie Mae talked to her as Mamma would have talked, and then, as if it had only waited for the cleansing of hate, had come her chance. Through Papa of all people. That was the strangest part of all. She had tried to give the credit to Mr. Tom Shane, but it was Papa really who had come round and given it to her.

The shadows had lengthened when Enie walked to the house. She roused Jenny and sponged the heat rash on her neck and sent her to play in the cool. She got into an old dress she didn't intend to take to Mills Falls, put on a pair of Henry Jim's outgrown sneakers and went for a walk. From the edge of the west field she could see Shanes' chimneys; they rose above the rounded tops of the ancient oaks, immutable against the summer sky. Would she be free of Shanes when she set out on the road to her own life? Did she want to be? She could not answer these questions and she retraced her steps to the house, hurrying because the afternoon had become evening and she feared Jenny might tire of her play and stray in search of company.

She climbed the lot fence and was back in the yard again. She opened the woodshed door and looked in. She could just make out in the dimness the strap handing on the wall—the strap that had kept the young Singletons in check and sent T.H. from home too soon. Enie moved swiftly into the shed and took the strap from its nail. It was cobwebby and stiff, dried with age and long disuse. She ran out the door with it and hurled it into the distance. It fell somewhere in the dog fennel beyond the lot. Wiping the dust from her hands, she breathed a sigh.

She walked round the yard, rested her palm against the fig tree, looked up at the spread branches of the mulberry. In the front yard she plucked a sprig of larkspur from Mamma's flower bed and stuck it in her hair. Stooping, she touched the thick green glass of a bottle in the walk's border.

Jenny, leaving the swing, stood to watch, large-eyed. "What are you looking for, Enie?" Enie laughed and hugged her. She couldn't tell Jenny she was saying good-by to all that belonged to her past. All but the graves at Pleasant Grove; Enie knew she would never again try to reach Mamma through the moldering earth.

Leeroy came from the woods, Henry Jim came home and did the chores. Enie set supper on the table; before Jenny went to sleep, she read her a story from Leeroy's reader. While the water heated for her bath, she sat on the porch and listened to the insects' churring. Just over the field, across the road, the moon came up, silver-white in the dark blue sky. Enie watched it climb slowly and steadily till it hung between the dark mound of the chinaberry tree and the taller dark of the oak, clear and bright as a promise.

21

E<small>NIE LOOKED</small> round to make sure she had not left anything unpacked, feeling the tug of the room's emptiness under the rapid beating of her heart. Jenny slept soundly, her body a small mound beneath the sheet, her face turned to the wall. Enie tiptoed to the bed and leaned over, wanting to kiss Jenny but afraid of waking her. The scent of boiling coffee stole through the house, and Enie crept in her stockinged feet to the boys' room, her high-heeled pumps in her hand.

Henry Jim was half out of bed, a leg trailing the floor, while Leeroy took up two-thirds of the space. Enie looked at her brothers, hating to wake Henry Jim. But it was daylight and she was nervous about the bus. Her body was tight as a fiddlestring and little prickles of apprehension kept darting up and down her back. She laid a hand on

Henry Jim's shoulder. "Get up, Henry Jim, it's after five."

Henry Jim cracked an eye open, then the other. His sleep-dulled gaze wandered uncomprehendingly over Enie, but he struggled up and shook his head as if he had come out of water. He looked big and tough in his underdrawers, the muscles rippling under the sunburnt skin of his arms.

"Don't make any fuss," Enie warned in a whisper. "I don't want the kids to wake up." She looked at Leeroy, thin and knobby as he had been when he slept with her, only much longer, his face pinched and delicate as ever, his shaggy hair darkly bunched on the lumpy pillow. Henry Jim rolled out and reached for his jeans. Enie turned away and went to the kitchen.

The room was still dim with early morning, but a brightness was fanning out from the east over wet leaves and the night-cooled earth. While Henry Jim did the milking, Enie dragged her trunk out of Mamma's room into the kitchen. She wished she could stop shaking. When she and Henry Jim sat down she could not drink her coffee. Henry Jim supped his noisily. "You better eat," he advised. "You're liable to feel mighty holler before you get there."

Enie pushed a bit of biscuit between her teeth. "I never could eat when I was going somewheres," she admitted faintly. Henry Jim sniggered.

"Reckon you haven't been anywheres often enough to starve you to death," he said.

The clock with the crack across its face ticked the minutes off in a wheezy voice. Time was flying, and now that the hour had come it was all Enie could do to go. All of her seemed to be shrinking, pulling back, back to her beginnings and a time that was gone forever. Henry Jim pushed his chair back, wiped his mouth on his sleeve and said, sounding like Papa, "We better get a move on."

Enie made a flustered motion toward the dishes, but Henry Jim said, "I can clear up whenever I get back." He jerked his head toward the clock. "Twenty to six; we got to get going if you aim to ketch that six o'clock bus."

Enie picked up her new purse. It was shiny imitation patent leather with a fine fancy brass clasp. It felt slippery in her hands and she clutched it till her fingers ached. She was cold in her thin blouse and wished she had worn the one Miss Elsie Mae had given her. Henry Jim heaved the trunk onto his shoulder and strode out of the house with it. Enie lingered, looking blankly about the kitchen. Wood crackled softly in the stove, the clock ticked, a fly found the lip of the syrup pitcher and settled down to drink. Enie tightened her grip on her purse and bolted from the kitchen.

Henry Jim slammed the tailboard behind the trunk and climbed into the cab. Enie carefully settled her skirt round her and pulled up her stockings. Her feet felt cramped already in the graduation pumps. Henry Jim pressed the starter. The motor snorted, belched and died in a reek of gasoline. Henry Jim dropped a brief "durn" and bore his thumb down on the starter, yanked the choke. The motor snorted again, spat, began to cough and roar. Henry Jim backed viciously, swung round and drove out into the road.

The sun was up now, fiery and hazy over the fields. It was going to be a hot day, like all summer days in Tired Creek. Rays struck through the cab of the truck, touching Enie's freckled arms and Henry Jims' freckled cheek, catching bright gleams from the two red heads. Sand sprayed out from the truck tires.

Signs of life showed in the houses—Vances', Elkins'; and over to the left, back from the road, a line of smoke rose from a chimney at Howells'. Ahead of them Shanes' house gleamed its spring coat of paint through the trees. Enie pictured Ralph still sleeping, and something flashed over her heart and was gone, lost in the terrible excitement of going away.

Where the rough country road ran into the paved highway just beyond Miss Katy's store, Henry Jim pulled up on the shoulder. He flung his door open and leaped to the ground. Enie fumbled at the broken catch of her door, pushed it open with her knee and hopped down. She watched Henry Jim take the trunk out of the back of the pickup. The morning air stirred the hair on her neck, the grass was wet with dew under her feet. What if the clock had been wrong, the bus already gone?

As if he sensed her terror, Henry Jim said soothingly, "You got plenty time."

Enie sat on her trunk and Henry Jim stamped about restlessly, rolling a cigarette, kicking at the grass on the roadside. A car went speeding up the highway, then another. A pair of dusty sparrows picked at mule droppings in the dirt road. Enie held tightly to her purse. A multitude of petty things began to hound her: Had she done all she had meant to do? Had she left enough clean clothes for Leeroy and Jenny, so Miss Elsie Mae would not have to do a washing right away? Would Leeroy and Jenny be all right? Oh, Leeroy and Jenny . . .

A muffled humming rose on the morning quiet, grew louder, became a swelling roar of power, of things unknown, of new and terrifying life—long yearned-for and now unfolding too quickly.

"Here she comes," Henry Jim announced, and throwing a helpless, frightened look at him, Enie saw his face touched with more than sunlight, touched with a haze of longing. Henry Jim, the farmer, the stolid, the contented, the undreaming— Henry Jim wanted to go on the bus! Then he turned, wildly signaling, and she could not see his face. She got up off the trunk, all feeling centered dreadfully in the middle of her chest.

The bus loomed, enormous, bigger, it seemed, than anything Enie had ever encountered, bearing down upon her, flattening and obliterating the life behind her as it might the luckless body of a cat in the road. It came to a standstill, its brake sneezing. The great door swung open, the driver stepped to the ground. "O.K., Sis," he said, and fished a big crank from the floor of the bus. "Where to?"

"Mills Falls," Enie said, and the driver began to open the side of the bus. He and Henry Jim moved the trunk into the yawning cavity, the door clapped down, the driver twisted the crank and withdrew it, tossing it through the door onto the floor. "Three-forty-two," he said, and Enie laid a five dollar bill in his hand.

She was dimly aware of the faces at the windows high above her as she dropped her change into her purse and carefully fastened the clasp. The driver touched her elbow politely, saying something about changing in Andalusia as she stepped up. Her heart was banging so hard it might suffocate her and her face was tingling with heat. A woman, tired-faced and stringy-haired, dandled a baby. A man slept, his mouth wide open. Enie took the first vacant seat, next to a window, and saw Henry Jim standing below her, squinting against the sun. He raised his hand and she saw the bit of rag tied about a finger he had cut a day or two ago.

The bus driver dragged the great lever into low gear and Enie lifted her hand, tried to smile at Henry Jim. As the bus began to move, she saw his head jerk round away from her. She pressed her face to the window, waving frantically, feeling the last of all that was known to her slipping out of her grasp. She saw Papa then, come running up to

Henry Jim and stand panting beside him. Papa had come to see her off, to say good-by, maybe to wish her luck . . . She half stood, fumbling at the window catch that would not budge. If only Papa had got here sooner, if only . . . if only . . .

The bus ground into second gear, shuddered, plunged, gathered speed, and Papa and Henry Jim and the pickup slid away behind her. Enie sank back into her seat. Tears were running down her face. She opened her purse to get her handkerchief, wiped her eyes and blew her nose as inconspicuously as she could. She took out the compact she'd bought on Saturday—a piece of tomfoolery Papa would not have approved of—and dabbed powder on the splotches tears had left under her eyes, fastened her purse and closed her fingers about it once more.

The bus was traveling fast now, its great tires singing on the concrete with a high whine. Pine trees and scrub oaks and dust-filmed blackberry bushes flashed by the window in the twinkling of an eye. Little unpainted houses like the Singletons' and bigger painted ones like the Howells' slid by and were lost. Through an open window across the aisle wind fanned softly in, lifting Enie's hot red hair. Her heart lifted too, as though on wings. Past the driver, through the big windshield she saw the road ahead like a great funnel, its small end widening to let the bus through.